Mother of the Most High

A Historical Novel

Mother *of the* Most High

DEBORAH E. KAYE

Printed in Canada

ISBN: 978-1-4866-0954-3

Word Alive Press
131 Cordite Road, Winnipeg, MB R3W 1S1
www.wordalivepress.ca

MIX
Paper from responsible sources
FSC® C016245

Cataloguing in Publication information may be obtained through Library and Archives Canada

dedication

To my husband, Dennis, my soul mate,
my cheering section, and my best friend,
and
To my sons, Ian, David and Brian,
who taught me all it means to be a mother.

acknowledgments

Thank you to:

Kylee Unrau, for shocking me into action.

My invisible, unnamed, behind the scenes editor. I have enjoyed working with you!

Lynne Smith, for your belief in my abilities and for allowing me freedom of expression, with just the right amount of guidance and "pull" on the reins.

Grandson Jake, for your amazing artistic abilities and your willingness to share in my joy and dream.

My sister Susan Gibson, for memories of growing up and sharing in writing stories together and for your advice and encouragement through the past several years, for blazing the trail and showing me it was possible to share our words with the world and survive.

My pastor, Rev. Wayne Johnson, and his dear wife, Carol, who have given such encouragement for my writing.

My church family at Hebron Baptist in Nova Scotia, for putting up with my writings and ramblings every week.

My dear parents, Stewart and Kathleen Taylor, for instilling in me a love of reading and writing for as long as I can remember.

one

Shouts from the village filtered through the walls of the home Mary shared with her parents, Anna and Joses. Mary could see fear in Anna's eyes.

"We need to go!" Mary insisted as her mother held back.

Anna held Mary's arm, forcing her to slow down. As they approached the edge of the crowd, they could see Roman soldiers in the center, one with a firm grip on a young woman's arm.

Mary gasped, "That's Rebekah!"

Both Rebekah and her mother were crying and struggling. Rebekah was struggling to get away from the soldier; her mother was struggling to get to her daughter.

Joses appeared beside Mary and took her other arm as Mary made a move to get to her friend. "Stay here. There's nothing you can do for her! If you try to help, they'll take you as well."

Rebekah's mother gave one last agonizing scream and collapsed to the ground as the soldier rode off with her daughter.

Mary tore her arms out of the grip of her parents and ran in the opposite direction, for the hills behind the village.

"How long, O LORD? Will you forget me forever? How long will you hide your face from me? How long must I wrestle with my thoughts and every day have sorrow in my heart? How long

will my enemy triumph over me?" The words from the psalmist, David, ran through Mary's mind as she sat alone on the side of the hill, her arms resting on her knees. Her heart was heavy as she looked out over the village, so quiet and still now in the late afternoon light. Everyone she knew was living in fear as the Roman soldiers became more numerous.

"O God, we're Jews, Your chosen people. Why do these people think they can come in here and tell us what to do? Why do we need to pay taxes to Caesar? Can't You help us?" Her cry to God came from the depths of her sorrow.

The noise and confusion of the morning echoed in her ears. The soldiers had taken her friend Rebekah to be a slave in a Roman household because her father could not pay his taxes. The memory of Rebekah's terrified ashen face and her mother's screams were burned into her memory.

Again the words of the psalm came to her mind, and she gave voice to them. *"Look on me and answer me, O LORD my God. Give light to my eyes, or I will sleep in death; my enemy will say, 'I have overcome him,' and my foes will rejoice when I fall."*

She buried her head on her arms and sobbed, "O God, have You forgotten us?"

The breeze began to stir gently, and calmness came upon her as the remaining words of the psalm flowed through her mind. *"But I trust in your unfailing love; my heart rejoices in your salvation. I will sing to the LORD, for he has been good to me."*

She lifted her head as she heard footsteps approaching. Her mother, out of breath and her face flushed, came into sight around the boulder.

"There you are, Mary! You must come at once!" Anna sank onto a good-sized rock. "Just let me catch my breath first."

"Why do we need to get back right away? What's happened? Is everything all right?" Mary's words stumbled over each other in her hurry to find out the worst.

"Joseph has come to talk to your father," Anna replied. "I'll explain in a minute when I can breathe again."

Within a few minutes Anna was ready to go, but not without voicing her concerns. "Mary, why do you always come up here when you're upset? Why don't you stay with us where it's safe?"

As they started back toward the village Mary took Anna's hand. "Mother, I feel as though I must get away by myself to talk to God about it. I don't want to be around people when I'm upset."

"I always find that working hard helps me get through bad things," Anna replied.

"I know you do, Mother, but I'm not like you in that way," Mary said. "I have to get by myself to work things out quietly."

Her mother squeezed her hand. "No, you are not like me. You are like your father. I am very thankful for that!"

Suddenly Mary remembered her mother's earlier words. She asked, "Why has Joseph come to see Father? Why is it so important for me to be there?"

"He heard that the Roman soldiers took Rebekah this morning, and he knows your father doesn't have enough money for his taxes. If Joseph pays the bride price and marries you, you won't be taken as a Roman slave. You need to be there so they can finish their agreement," Anna replied.

Mary's breath caught in her throat. "I'm to be a bride? Joseph's bride?"

Anna stopped and wrapped her arms around her daughter. "Mary, Joseph is a good man. He cares a great deal about you, about our family. He's a hard worker, and he, too, is looking for the deliverance."

"But Mother, I don't feel ready to be a bride!" Mary protested.

Anna smiled her reassurance. "This is just the betrothal. We have a year to get you ready to be a bride."

They hurried through the village to their home.

After they entered the house and Mary's eyes became adjusted to the dim light, she could make out the forms of her father, Joses, Joseph, one of their neighbors, and the rabbi from the synagogue.

Joseph stood with the shtar in his hand. With his voice trembling he read, "On this third day of the week, the fifteenth day of the month Cheshvan in the year 3763 since the creation of the world according to the reckoning that we are accustomed to using here in the town of Nazareth in Galilee, I, Joseph son of Jacob of the family of Judah, say to this maiden Mary, daughter of Joses, also of the family of Judah, 'Be thou my wife according to the law of Moses and Israel.'

"I will work for you, honor, provide for, and support you, in accordance with the practice of Jewish husbands, who work for their wives, honor, provide for, and support them in truth.

"I will betroth you forever. I will betroth you with righteousness and justice and with goodness and mercy."

Joseph and Mary shared a glass of wine; then Joseph passed Mary the ring. She accepted it, showing that she was accepting Joseph as her betrothed husband.

The summer sun was already hot early the next morning as Mary poked her head out the door of her home. Would she see Joseph today? She had mixed feelings. She was pleased that she was betrothed, but he was so much older than she was. He was twenty-seven to her fourteen—nearly twice her age—but he was a kind man. He had been almost apologetic when he came to talk to her father. He would make a good husband. He shared her beliefs in the one true God. They shared the same opinion about the oppression of the Jews by the Romans; it was time for deliverance from the Caesars, in particular from Caesar Augustus, whose long arm reached their small town, all the way from Rome, in the persons of his soldiers and tax collectors.

Mary's thoughts turned to the prophecies she had heard from the Scriptures. "*The virgin will be with child…*" For as long as she could remember it had been impressed upon all the girls that one of them could be the "chosen vessel" if she kept herself pure. Now that she was betrothed to Joseph and soon to be a married woman, there was no chance that she would be chosen. She sighed as she left the house with her water jug and made her way to the well at the far end of the village.

She was later than usual this morning. No one else was out. There had been no rain for a while, and the dust was thick along the path to the well. Rocks were so close to the surface that the sparse grass didn't have much chance to provide any contrasting color to the unending brown. How the heat shimmered! It had never been this bad before. She couldn't take her eyes off the shimmering light beside the well.

"Greetings, Mary," a voice said from the midst of the light.

Mary's heart pounded. She stood without moving, scarcely breathing. What was going on?

The form of a man in pure white garments took shape. "Don't be afraid. You have found favor with God," he continued. "He has blessed you and chosen you to be the mother of His Son. You are to name Him Jesus."

"Am I dreaming?" Mary whispered. "How could this happen? I'm not married yet. I'm still a virgin. How could I have a child?"

"This Child will be God's Son. The Holy Spirit will impregnate you. Your cousin Elisabeth, the wife of Zacharias the priest, is now six months pregnant with the one who will be the herald of your son. God is able to accomplish this. Nothing is impossible with Him."

"I will do as the Lord requires. May His will be done." She managed this much before her dry mouth and trembling voice overcame her ability to speak. Immediately the light was gone, and with it, the angel.

Her hands were shaking as she drew the water from the well. She sat on the edge of the well for a few minutes until she was sure her legs would hold her, and then she made her way back down the dusty path to the house. Her mind had not yet fully grasped what had just happened. She set the water jug inside the door where her mother would find it and retreated to the shade at the back of the house where she could sit and think.

Her eyes sought the far horizon, beyond the hills to the west, where she knew the Great Sea lay.

When would it happen? How would she know? Was she allowed to tell anyone? What about Joseph?

"Mary! Where are you? Her mother's voice broke through her reverie. "Come help me with this water jug."

"Coming." Mary glanced down at her abdomen. *Am I pregnant now? Who should I tell first? If it were Joseph's child I would tell him, but...*

She decided to wait until she could put her thoughts more easily into words before she shared her good news with anyone. Her hand rested lightly on her abdomen as she walked into the house.

As soon as she approached her mother, she blurted out her news. "Mother, I'm going to have a baby."

Anna whirled around. Her eyes were snapping with anger, her brows drawn together.

"How could you? And Joseph seemed like such an

honorable man! Shame on you, Mary. Shame on you!"

"But Mother, Joseph isn't the father."

"Mary!" Tears coursed down Anna's cheeks. "What have you done, child?"

"Mother, it really isn't what you think."

"You are betrothed to a man; you tell me you are pregnant and that he isn't the father. How could it be anything but what I think?"

"I saw an angel. He was at the well this morning. He told me I was the one chosen to be the mother of God's Son. He said I had found favor with God. Isn't that wonderful?"

Anna dropped heavily to the bench inside the door. "She's gone mad," she whispered.

Mary knelt on the floor and placed her hands over her mother's, stilling their nervous twisting. "Mother, we've been told about the coming of the Messiah. We all know He'll come someday. We all know that a virgin will have this child. I hoped it would be me, but I really didn't think it would be. God has chosen me, your daughter, to bear His Son!"

"How?"

"The angel told me."

"Just stop with 'the angel'! I mean, how can I believe you?"

"Mother, you know me better than anyone else does. Do I look as though I'm lying?"

"No, but if you are mad—"

"I'm not mad."

Anna studied her face, taking in the dark hair framing the perfectly formed face; the nose that was just slightly crooked; the mouth, so mobile, so ready to laugh and smile; the wide-set dark eyes, with a sparkle of excitement in them.

"I have always known when you were telling me the truth. Your eyes are always so honest. They seem clear and sane.

But, the mother of the Messiah? The mother of our king? My daughter? Why you?"

"Why not me?" Mary countered.

"It's so unbelievable."

"I know it is."

"You know." Her mother studied her face again as she spoke softly. "You *do* know. My daughter will be the mother of the Messiah."

She reached out and took Mary's face in her hands. Then she leaned forward and kissed her daughter. Their arms wrapped closely around each other.

"Mother, will Joseph believe me?"

"Of course he will. He loves you."

"You didn't at first."

"I do now. It will probably take some time, but he will."

"How do I tell Father?" she asked.

"We will tell him together," her mother promised.

After their evening meal Anna spoke to Joses. "We need to talk to you. Something happened to Mary today. An angel spoke with her when she went for water and told her she is God's chosen vessel for bearing our Messiah."

Joses sat for a few seconds, stroking his beard with his right hand. His dark eyes met Mary's. "How did you know it was an angel?" His voice was calm and quiet, rather than accusing.

Mary replied, "He didn't walk. He just appeared in a bright light."

"Can you remember what he said?"

"Yes, Father. I remember every word! I don't think I will ever forget! He said, 'Don't be afraid. You have found favor with God. He has blessed you and chosen you to be the mother of His Son. You are to name Him Jesus.'"

Joses stood and put his arms around both Mary and Anna.

"O God, You have promised us a deliverer. You are now fulfilling that promise through our daughter, Mary. We ask for Your help, for Your strength and Your guidance as we go through this and as Mary carries this special child. Protect her and the child. Amen."

Mary didn't see Joseph that day. She and her parents spent time talking, pondering, and going over the Scriptures they could remember about the coming of the Messiah. Mary shared with them the news about Elisabeth.

"I've heard rumors about that," her father replied. "Some are saying she has a terrible disease; some say Zacharias's inability to speak is somehow related to it."

"I'd like to go see her," Mary said. "We have a lot to talk about."

"We'll see."

The next afternoon Joseph arrived unexpectedly at the door of the house. Mary invited him to join her on the bench beside the house, away from the sun.

"Joseph, I have something important to tell you." Mary studied his face carefully before she continued. "We've talked about the coming of the Messiah and how He will deliver Israel from oppression. We've talked about how and when He will come. Yesterday an angel came to me and told me that God has chosen me to be the mother of the Messiah."

"How could I be the father of the Messiah?"

"You aren't. God is."

Joseph's eyes darkened as she saw the unbelief growing.

"And when is all this to take place?"

"As far as I know, it already has."

"As far as you know?" Joseph's voice was getting louder and sharper. "What's *that* supposed to mean?"

"I've never had an angel visit me before," Mary replied. "I've never been pregnant before, either. I don't know how it is going to feel at first."

"You're pregnant?" Joseph stood up abruptly.

"If I'm going to be the mother of the Messiah, then I have to be pregnant."

"How did that happen?"

"The angel said."

"Are you sure it was an *angel*?" he snapped.

She bit back a sharp retort and forced herself to answer calmly and quietly. "Yes. He just appeared, in light. He told me that my cousin Elisabeth is pregnant with the one who will be the herald of this baby. He told me I had found favor with God and that I was chosen to bear His Son. I asked how that was going to happen since I'm a virgin, and he said the Holy Spirit would look after that."

Joseph shook his head, then shrugged his shoulders. He opened his mouth but said no words. He raised his hands as though to help articulate what he was trying to say. Finally, he strode off without saying another word.

Mary remained on the bench. Hurt, anger and compassion churned in her. She clasped her hands in her lap and sat with her head hanging.

I will do as the Lord requires. May His will be done. The memory of the words she had spoken came to her as forcefully as if she had just spoken them.

She looked up as she felt the presence of another person. Her mother sat down beside her and placed her arm around Mary's shoulders.

"Give him a little time, Mary. He will be back. This is harder for him than it was for you or for me."

"Perhaps I'm on my own for this." Mary's voice trembled.

"What man would be willing to marry a woman who is pregnant with a child that is not his?"

"You'd be surprised how many," Anna replied.

"But I was thinking," Mary continued. "The Scriptures say that a virgin shall conceive and bear a son. How could a woman marry and continue to be a virgin? Would any man be willing to take a wife and let her remain a virgin?"

Her mother thought before she spoke. "It would take a very special man, one who loved his wife more than he loved himself."

Mary replied slowly, "He would have to be one of God's own choosing, wouldn't he?"

Two days passed without a word from Joseph. On the third day he arrived at the house early in the morning, before Mary had even made the trip to the well. Mary studied his face. His brow was not furrowed with worry. His eyes, so dark and deep-set, looked into hers with no shadow of anger or suspicion. In fact, they were overflowing with love and respect.

"May I help you draw water this morning, Mary?"

After she nodded, he picked up the water jug, and they set off toward the well. For most of the trip they were both silent. Then Joseph spoke.

"Mary, I'm sorry I doubted your word. You have always been honest with me. You have never given me any cause for jealousy. When you told me that you were going to have a child—*the* child—I should have believed you without question, but I'm human. It took a visit from an angel to convince me too."

Mary slipped her hand into Joseph's, and he squeezed it gently.

"I had a dream. At least I think it was a dream," Joseph said. "The angel told me not to be afraid to marry you. He told me that God is the Father of the child you are carrying. He even told me His name is to be Jesus."

Mary gasped. "He told me the same thing!" Her tears spilled down over her cheeks. "God is good. He is not going to make me face this alone."

"Can we marry right away, instead of waiting? I wouldn't want people thinking…well, you know what they would think."

"Joseph, do you know what this involves?" Mary asked.

"Yes, I do. We won't be able to consummate our marriage until after the child is born."

"And you are willing?"

"For God and for you, yes, I am willing. I think if God has asked us to do this, He will also give us the ability to carry it out."

Joseph talked to Joses about their plans for moving the wedding date up.

"Joseph, I agree that it is best for the both of you; but because of the political situation in the country, we should tell told no one about the angel or why you are changing the wedding date. The people are going to think what they are going to think. It is better to bear a little scandal than to have the life of our Messiah put in danger."

The people did make their own guesses, smiling behind their hands or whispering when they thought none of the family was in earshot. It was not lost on Mary or her mother. As they made their way to and from the well, they could hear the whispered comments.

"Couldn't wait to take her as his wife!"

"Do they think anyone is fooled by the change of date?"

"Count off the time. See if it adds up."

Sometimes the conversations would be cut off as they approached, and their neighbors would look anywhere but at them.

"I want to slap their gossiping silly faces!" her mother blurted out in a moment when the two of them were alone.

"Mother, we know the truth. Let it go. Think of the danger there could be if the truth got to the authorities that a king was going to be born. Just keep that in mind and smile when you want to scream." Mary gave her mother a hug and went to join Joseph.

In a week's time, which they needed for the required traditions, Joseph and Mary were married in the chupah. Mary wore an embroidered blue tunic and robe, while Joseph wore an ornate wedding robe, embroidered in several different colors, suitable for a man of his age and standing. After the guests had all departed, Mary and Joseph sat hand in hand, talking. They talked about the week-long celebrations and preparations, the guests who had been present, their hopes for their future together and the child that Mary now carried. Mary squeezed Joseph's hand and sighed.

"I wonder how Elisabeth is doing," she whispered.

"Why don't you go visit her and see?"

"You'd let me? So soon after the wedding?"

"It would probably be best. It would be easier for me to keep my promise to God if you were not here. I will see if there is anyone going that way in the next little while with whom you could travel."

two

Within a week Joseph had made arrangements for Mary to travel with a family on their way to Jerusalem. They agreed that she would stay until Elisabeth no longer needed her.

The sky was heavy with clouds on the morning they set out. Mary thought it was fitting, since she was leaving her husband for several months. She gave him a hug and turned toward the road before he could see the tears in her eyes. She didn't want to know if he was feeling the same yet thought it would be worse to find out that he wasn't. She hoisted her bundle of clothing and food to her shoulder and joined the family.

The first part of the road led down along the side of the mountains overlooking the Valley of Jezreel. Mary rejoiced in the vistas of vineyards on the far slopes, the olive groves, and the nearer views of green grass dotted with the white of sheep. In the early morning, she could still see dew on the grass, and she took deep breaths of the freshness of the day. Occasionally she could hear the trickle of a stream running close beside the road. She was young, strong and healthy and was able and willing to help with the four little ones, whose ages ranged from five years to a few months. They tired quickly, often needing to be carried. The rest stops were frequent for feeding, for settling squabbles and for resting tired arms after carrying the smallest ones.

The five-year-old, a girl named Sarah with large dark eyes, long dark hair and a sweet smile, took a special liking to Mary and walked with her, holding her hand when she wasn't otherwise engaged with the other children. Mary loved the feel of the soft little hand nestled so comfortably and trustingly in hers. As small as she was, Sarah carried her own bundle of provisions and helped with the little ones during the rest times. She chattered incessantly about her little brothers, Joshua, who was four, Joel, who was two, and "her" baby, Benjamin.

"And, Mary? Do you know where we are going?"

Mary smiled down at the little girl. "Well, I know I am going to visit my cousin. Where are you going?"

"My daddy says we are going to live with his mama; that's our grandmother, you know. Daddy's Papa died, so we are going to help Grandmother make pots."

Mary glanced over at Sarah's mother, Deborah, an adult version of her daughter.

"David is a potter, like his father was," she explained with a smile.

She adjusted baby Benjamin a little higher in the sling, prompting Mary to ask, "Do you want me to carry him for a bit? You must be getting tired."

Deborah shook her head. "If I give him to you, either Joshua or Joel will want to take his place." They both looked back at David, carrying Joel on his back and holding Joshua by the hand.

As they traveled farther south, the roads became rough and dusty. Every time soldiers came along, they had to quickly move off the road or risk being trampled. Mary grew increasingly tired and tense as they traveled through the twisting part of the road that led through rocky areas. They were always listening for the sounds of marching feet or horses' hooves, warning of the approach of the soldiers. Sometimes the echoes of marching drove them from the road long before the soldiers came into sight. When that happened, they sat quietly, had something to eat or simply allowed the children to rest.

At night, if there were no other travelers, they built a fire well away from the road, with the adults taking turns keeping watch. If they were in company with other travelers, the men kept watch, allowing the women to sleep.

The journey lasted for a week, and it was with a thankful heart that Mary bade David, Deborah, and their children, especially Sarah, good-bye a short distance from Elisabeth's house in the hills outside Jerusalem. She walked quickly, now that she no longer had a child on her hip or hanging from her skirt. She smiled to herself, thinking that soon she would have a child of her own to follow her around.

She entered the outskirts of the village as the day was cooling to evening. The homes here were larger than in Nazareth. She knew that as a priest, Zacharias had more money than her parents did. She admired the small gardens as she made her way through the unfamiliar street, thankful that her mother had described Elisabeth's house to her. It was unmistakable when she saw it, set apart from the other houses on the street, with its courtyard surrounded by olive and fig trees.

"Elisabeth!" she called as she approached. "It's Mary. I bring greetings from Mother and Father."

Elisabeth turned quickly at the sound of Mary's voice and spoke loudly. "You are praised among all women, and I praise the child you are carrying! Why should the mother of my Lord come to visit me? As soon as I heard you speak, my baby leaped for joy. How happy is she that believed! God will accomplish those things about which He told her."

Mary was overcome by a joy she had never before experienced. She raised her hands in the air and praised God for choosing her from among all the women in the world to be the mother of His Son.

The cousins exchanged hugs and looked one another over to see the changes that had occurred since they had last seen each other six years before. Mary noted with contentment that Elisabeth's eyes still sparkled with fun, even though there were a few wrinkles showing at the corners. She noticed, too, a few white strands in her otherwise dark hair.

"Come in, come into the house. You must be so tired. Tell me all the news of the village. Do Joanna and Ruth still gossip at the well?" Elisabeth pulled Mary into her home.

Mary became aware of her surroundings as Elisabeth's chatter continued. She felt as though her feet, unaccustomed to tile, might slip on the smooth floor and was relieved when Elisabeth led her to a chair to sit down. She wondered what Elisabeth would say to living again in a home with a packed-earth floor.

Elisabeth had been like a dear auntie when Mary was a little girl, but she had met Zacharias only a few times, so she didn't know him as well. To Mary, Zacharias seemed much older than Elisabeth. His hair was more liberally sprinkled with white, and his hands had the unmistakable marks of an older man—the veins stood out noticeably. Through the evening the three of them became reacquainted. It had been many years since Mary had attended the wedding between the older couple, and since they lived so far apart, there had been no opportunity to visit. Even though Zacharias was unable to talk, he could still communicate through gestures and smiles. Mary was warmed by his love for Elisabeth; it came through clearly, with no words needed.

As the two women exchanged memories of their years together, Zacharias placed his hand on Elisabeth's shoulder to get her attention. He raised his eyebrows as he lifted an imaginary cup to his mouth. Elisabeth squeezed his hand and replied, "Thank you, Zacharias. We would love to have a drink."

Zacharias returned a short time later, carrying a tray with three goblets filled with a dark red wine. Mary enjoyed the coolness of the liquid in her mouth. The thought ran unbidden through her head, *Even their wine tastes better than ours!*

Elisabeth told Mary about the visit of an angel to Zacharias and the declaration of the angel that the baby's name was to be John. Mary told them about her visitation from an angel, who had told her about Elisabeth.

Zacharias made signs to Elisabeth. "You want me to tell her his name?" she asked.

Zacharias nodded, and Elisabeth turned to Mary. "The angel told Zacharias his name was Gabriel."

Mary gasped. "He was the same one who talked to me!"

Zacharias reached out and clasped her hand, smilingly acknowledging their similar experiences. The discomfort she had initially felt in his presence disappeared, and they were able to communicate easily, even without Elisabeth's help.

The days and weeks preceding the birth of Elisabeth's son were filled with laughter and chatter, the hopes for the future always present in their thoughts, if not in their conversation. Elisabeth, in spite of her advanced age for childbearing, was full of vigor, needing only brief rests before taking on another task. She and Mary often walked together for exercise. They wouldn't travel very far at a time—just enough to keep them from getting lazy, Elisabeth would often say with a smile. Occasionally they visited with Elisabeth's neighbor Sarah.

"She's the only one who isn't afraid to visit me," Elisabeth explained. "So many of the other women think that Zacharias and I must have done something terrible for God to have taken away Zacharias's voice. They think I have some dreadful disease and am not really with child. I've heard them talking. They think God is judging us for our sin."

"Have you tried to explain?" Mary asked.

"Did you explain your situation to people?" Elisabeth countered. "They will find out when the baby is born. I really don't need to be vindicated. God knows the truth."

Mary chuckled. "I was always telling Mother that it didn't matter what people thought about me, and now here I am saying just what she said!"

One day as they sat preparing baby garments they touched on a topic they had not covered previously.

"Elisabeth, do you ever question why God chose you?"

"How do you mean that?"

"Well, not in a complaining or a proud way, but more in a humbled way. Like, 'Why did God choose me? Isn't there someone else more qualified?'— I'm not finding fault. I just don't understand."

Elisabeth sat quietly for a few seconds and then smiled slightly. "Yes, I question Him. I feel honored, but very much humbled. I am thankful He chose me, but, like you, I don't understand."

"He doesn't really ask us to understand, though," Mary replied. "He just asks us to be obedient."

Elisabeth reached out and placed her hand on Mary's. "I know why He chose you to be the mother of His Son. You can accept by faith the things that He asks you to do."

"Oh, but Elisabeth, sometimes I get so scared! What if I make a terrible mistake? What if I don't know what I am supposed to do?"

"Mary, God knows you," Elisabeth said gently. "He made you. Do you think He would let you make a terrible mistake with His Son? You don't have to do it all at once. Take just one day, one moment, at a time."

As Mary reached over to give Elisabeth a hug, Elisabeth gasped. Mary pulled back, startled. "Are you all right?"

"Just wait a minute and I'll let you know." She gasped again and clenched her fists. "Well, I've never given birth before, but I would say that I am about to find out what it is like."

Mary's eyes widened. "What do I do?"

"Go get Sarah."

Mary rushed to the next house, calling for Sarah as she ran.

Sarah came unhurriedly to the door. "There's no panic. Stop to catch your breath. It's not going to happen right away."

But Mary turned and fled back to Elisabeth. She found her standing by the table, clutching the edge for support.

"I always thought...I would have...time to prepare... myself." She groaned, and her knees began to buckle.

Mary grasped her around the waist and was able to get her to the bed.

By the time Sarah arrived, Mary had built up the fire and had some water heating, taking time to be thankful that Zacharias had seen that the water jugs were full before he left. Sarah busied herself with Elisabeth, so Mary took the opportunity to step outside.

She called to one of the young boys playing nearby. "Josiah, would you please go to the temple and tell Zacharias that it is time for Elisabeth to give birth? And please hurry." The boy trotted off obediently.

By the time Zacharias arrived three hours later, out of breath, Elisabeth was giving her final push. The strong cry of a newborn filled the house. Mary, Sarah and Elisabeth all laughed and cried simultaneously.

"He sounds angry!" laughed Sarah. She handed the crying newborn to Mary. "Here, you get him ready for his father to see while I see to his mother."

Mary's looked at Sarah in unbelief.

"Take your time; you'll do fine," Sarah assured her with a smile.

Mary took the squirming, howling newborn in her arms and carried him to the table, where she had prepared a soft pad for someone—anyone but her—to clean up the child. She placed him carefully on the table and washed him with the water she had heated. She started with the wrinkled red face and thatch of dark hair, then moved on to the strong looking chest and arms, right to the soles of the tiny feet, complete to the even tinier toes. He cried and kicked through the whole procedure. By the time she had him clean, she was drenched with perspiration and as weak as though she had been running a long distance. She wrapped him and took him to Zacharias. "Here is your son."

Zacharias reached out trembling arms to receive his one and only son.

"Will he be another Zacharias?" asked Sarah.

Zacharias shook his head.

"Oh, of course he will!" Sarah retorted, turning back to Elisabeth. She missed the expression of fierce determination on Zacharias's face. Mary quietly placed her hand on his arm and smiled her understanding.

The days that followed were a blur of wonder to Mary as she experienced the delights and responsibilities of handling a newborn baby. She looked ahead to her own child with a mixture of anticipation and dread. It was such an awesome responsibility with a normal child, but hers would be the Son of God! The human aspect of it scared her some as well, with the thoughts of Elisabeth's pain still fresh in her mind. She gave her thoughts and worry to God, telling Him that she was His willing handmaid, no matter what He asked of her. Through the silence, she felt His comforting presence assuring her that He would always be with her.

When the baby was eight days old, the neighbors and friends gathered for his circumcision and naming.

The sandek took the baby from Zacharias's arms and carried him to the table where the mohel stood. Mary and Elisabeth, because they were women, were not allowed near the table, so they stood together at the far side of the room. When the baby began to cry, Mary squeezed Elisabeth's hand.

The voice of the mohel could be heard over the crying of the baby. "Behold, I give him my covenant of peace. Preserve this child to his father and to his mother. The father of the righteous shall greatly rejoice, and he who fathers a wise child shall have joy from him. Your father and your mother shall be glad, and she who bore you shall rejoice."

The sandek returned the baby to Zacharias, who, with tears running down his face, carried him over to his mother.

Someone asked if he was to be named Zacharias, after his father.

Elisabeth replied, "No, he is to be called John."

The noise level increased dramatically as the words sank in.

"But there's no 'John' in the connection."

"It's not as though he'll ever have another son."

"Poor man can't speak for himself."

Zacharias motioned for them to bring him a writing tablet. On it, in a large, unmistakable hand, he wrote, "His name is John."

Then, in a clear voice that startled them because of his long silence, he began to speak. "Praise be to the Lord, the God of Israel, because he has come and has redeemed his people. He has raised up a horn of salvation for us in the house of his servant David (as he said through his holy prophets of long ago), salvation from our enemies and from the hand of all who hate us—to show mercy to our fathers and to remember his holy covenant, the oath he swore to our father Abraham: to rescue us from the hand of our enemies, and to enable us to serve him without fear in holiness and righteousness before him all our days.

"And you, my child, will be called a prophet of the Most High; for you will go on before the Lord to prepare the way for him, to give his people the knowledge of salvation through the forgiveness of their sins, because of the tender mercy of our God, by which the rising sun will come to us from heaven to shine on those living in darkness and in the shadow of death, to guide our feet into the path of peace."

Mary stood in awe and wonder as the meaning of the words registered in her mind. This baby, this tiny scrap of humanity, was going to proclaim deliverance to the world, to prepare the world for the coming of the Messiah—God's Son! Then with a shock she realized that the baby she was now carrying was the one for whom John would be making preparation.

The feast Mary and Elisabeth had prepared for the celebration following the circumcision was anticlimactic after Zacharias's miraculous recovery, but the neighbors stayed until late in the afternoon, eating and drinking and talking over the events of the day.

After the birth of John and the restoration of Zacharias's voice, the neighbors were no longer afraid to associate with the family. The women of the community, always eager to see and hold a new baby, promised so much help to Elisabeth that Mary realized her willing hands were no longer needed. She asked Zacharias to make arrangements for her to travel back to Nazareth. She had been away long enough. She wanted to see Joseph, to talk to him, to share the wonders of what she had witnessed, and to set up her own home before the birth of her baby.

three

A FEW DAYS LATER, MARY WAS ON HER WAY TO NAZARETH, walking home to her husband and family. The weather was considerably cooler, and there were no small children with the group, so they were able to cover greater distances in a day. Mary was healthy and strong; the baby was not yet evident, so she had no difficulty with the trip. As they grew closer and closer to Nazareth, her footsteps quickened, and she had to hold herself back to stay with the others.

What changes will I have to make in our home? she wondered; then she laughed at herself and her hurry. *I still have over five months before He's even born, and He won't be crawling around for a while after that. I'll give myself some time to get used to the idea of keeping my own home first, then suggest some changes to Joseph as I see the need.*

The day was approaching evening as they made their way into Nazareth. She hadn't told Joseph when she was coming, hoping to surprise him with a meal ready when he came in from his workshop. As she came within sight of the house, she could see Joseph sitting on the bench in front of the workshop.

Almost as soon as she saw him, he recognized her and came running to meet her. Before she could even speak, she was lifted off her feet and enveloped in a hug so tight she could hardly draw a breath.

"Joseph," she gasped, laughing, "let me breathe!"

He set her down but kept his hand on her shoulder as they walked the short distance to their home. "It is so good to see you again! I've missed you more than I imagined I would. If I had known before you went how much I would miss you, I probably wouldn't have been so eager for you to go."

As they entered the house she turned to him, burying her face in his chest, her arms tight around his waist. She relaxed against him as she felt his arms supporting her. It was wonderful to be held so close, to feel so cherished, to feel so much a part of this man, to know that they belonged to each other. They stood for many minutes, soaking up the joy of being together again.

Finally Mary pulled back a bit and looked up at Joseph. "Have you eaten your meal yet?"

He stared at her a moment. "Did I eat? I don't remember. I'm not hungry. I must have eaten. What did I have? I don't remember that either."

Mary laughed. "Well, I didn't eat, and I *am* hungry. Is there any food? Do you have any bread?"

"Yes, I have a bit of bread. Your mother took pity on me now and then, and she brought some bread this morning. Yes, I did eat! The bread is very good, but I left some. There is a bit of lamb left as well, and some fruit."

"Sounds better all the time!" Mary exclaimed.

"After all your traveling, you must be tired. Why don't you rest, and I can bring you your food?" Joseph suggested.

Mary's eyes widened, and her mouth fell open.

"It's just this once." Joseph added quickly, "I know you must be tired of being on your feet."

"Thank you, Joseph. I *am* tired. I wasn't finding fault; I just never, ever heard my father offer to serve my mother, no matter how tired she was. I love you so much." She reached up and kissed him on the cheek, prompting another hug before he turned to get her some food.

Through the evening they shared bits and pieces of their time apart. Joseph told her of the many orders he had received for his work and how busy he had been trying to keep up with the demand while at the same time trying to keep his standards high.

With excitement Mary related John's first cry and the wonder of new life, how tiny he was, yet how loud his voice of complaint. They laughed together over Elisabeth and Zacharias's fumbling attempts at bathing and caring for the tiny newborn.

"Will we be any better?" Joseph asked.

"Well, I've had a little practice," Mary replied, "and I will help you so that you will know what you are doing.

"Oh, Joseph, it was so amazing to see what God did! You know Zacharias couldn't speak before John was born, but as soon as he wrote that the baby's name was John, God restored his voice!"

Mary went to sleep early, tired out from the days she had spent walking from Jerusalem. Her first thoughts on awakening the next morning were confused. *Where am I? This doesn't look like Elisabeth's house. Am I in an inn? No, I am home!*

A great relief washed through her as she stretched her arms above her head and sat up. She could dimly see Joseph's outline in his bed across the room. He was still asleep.

She quietly arose and let herself out of the house to go get the water. The sun had not peeked above the horizon yet, but she could see the sky changing from pink to gold to silver. There were several other young women making their way to the village well. They greeted each other in quiet voices. Mary recognized two of her friends among them.

"When did you get back?" asked Rachel.

"How is Elisabeth?" asked Sarah.

"Did she really have a baby?" added Rachel.

"Joseph sure missed you!" Sarah said with a grin.

"I arrived home yesterday," Mary replied with a laugh. "Elisabeth is fine. Yes, she had a baby, a healthy boy. Come to my home later and I will tell you all about it."

Saying "my home" gave Mary a sense of pride. She held Sarah's comment that Joseph had missed her close to her heart. She filled her jug and headed for home. Her main desire today was to go see her mother. It had been so long since they had had a chance to just sit and talk. She had so many questions she wanted to ask about babies and her condition, what to expect and who to call and what to do. Her mind was spinning with a jumble of thoughts and questions.

By the time Joseph rose she had the fire going and breakfast cooking. This morning breakfast was a simple meal of oil-and-flour flat cakes and some dried figs. After he'd eaten he went into the workshop, where he was putting the finishing touches on a piece of furniture for one of the prominent businessmen of the village. Before noon he came in to let Mary know he was going to deliver the cabinet, and he would stop and let her mother know she was home.

A short while later she looked up to see her mother hurrying toward the house. Mary dashed out the door with her arms outstretched.

"Mary!" Anna exclaimed. "You're home! You're here! I missed you so much! You look better than you ever did. You are glowing!"

"With all the walking in the fresh air I have done in the last week, I'm really not surprised," Mary answered. She returned her mother's hug, then together they went into the house.

Mary was able to ask all the questions she could think of

and was assured by her mother that she would be right there for her.

"Oh, Mother, babies are such precious things! John was so helpless, and so soft. I could hardly feel his skin, it was so soft. And he smelled so good…most of the time."

Later that afternoon, Joseph found them deep in a discussion of the best ways to feed, bathe, dress, and train babies. Mary looked up as he came in. His eyes were dark with trouble.

"What is the matter, Joseph?" she asked.

"The Roman emperor wants to count us all—a census, they call it."

"That shouldn't be too bad, should it?" asked Anna.

"Everyone must go to the city of their ancestors for the census. That means I have to go to Bethlehem. And they have set the times when each of us must go. I have to be in Bethlehem in five months' time."

He looked steadily at Mary. She understood what he was trying to tell her. He would not be present when the baby was born. Her eyes grew wider, and she pressed her hands together in her lap.

"What happens if the baby comes as quickly as John did?" she asked in a small voice.

"You can just come back home while Joseph is away," Anna answered decisively. "You won't have to worry about a thing."

She reached over and gave her daughter a quick hug, then said her good-byes and headed for home.

Joseph sat on the bench beside Mary, and she leaned against him. "I just get back, and now it seems you are going away. Is our whole married life going to be like this?" Her voice was thick with unshed tears.

"I don't have to leave right away." He gave her a hug and laughed. "There is still a long time for you to get tired of me."

Throughout the rest of the day Mary was perturbed. She often found excuses to go into the workshop, where Joseph was fashioning another cabinet. On one occasion, Joseph looked at her, smiling.

"Come over here, Mary. I want to show you what I'm doing." He explained in intricate detail his plan for the cabinet. "I got more ideas as I worked on the last one. This one is going to be the best one I have ever made. I'm being very particular about all the fittings and joints. It will be held together perfectly well without nails or glue, but I'll use them as well.

"I'm going to keep it as a showpiece. It will be good to have examples of my work for strangers to see. I will fashion it to hold my tools, so I can take them with me when I'm traveling. That way, I won't have to be concerned about providing for myself while I'm away from the workshop."

They talked about the look and feel of the wood, the way it was cut, the process of finishing. Finally, Joseph said, "I'm beginning to remember some words from the scrolls. I think it was a reading from the prophet Micah. I will have to ask the rabbi about it, but it's been in my mind since I heard about the trip to Bethlehem. I think you're going to have to come with me."

"Why would I have to come with you? How could I come? I'm going to give birth!"

"As I recall, the old prophecy says that Bethlehem will be the birthplace of the Messiah. We could leave early enough that we would be there well ahead of when the baby is going to be born. Then we could find a place to live and get settled. I'll have my carpentry to provide for us, and we can stay until you and the child are able to travel back to Nazareth."

"My mother is not going to be pleased," Mary said.

"I will talk to the rabbi. If the scroll says the Messiah will be born in Bethlehem, she will not be able to argue."

Their eyes met and twinkled in fun. Together they said, "But you don't know my mother."

Mary laughed a little and then sighed. "I am so glad God gave me to you to look after. You know how to cheer me up. You know what makes me laugh. You know how to calm my fears. Just being close to you gives me a sense of peace and contentment."

Joseph turned from his workbench and hugged her. "Do you think that works only one way?" he asked. "I have never felt such contentment as when I'm holding you like this."

He kissed the top of her head.

"Tomorrow I will talk to the rabbi about the prophecy so we can begin to make preparations."

"You aren't going to tell him why you're asking, are you?" Mary asked in alarm.

"No, not unless God tells me to."

As promised, the next day Joseph stopped to talk to the rabbi about the prophet Micah. The rabbi, knowing that Joseph was of David's line, assumed that he was interested in the prophecy about Bethlehem because that was the town of his ancestors.

When Joseph arrived back home, Mary was waiting for him. "Yes, the Messiah is supposed to be born in Bethlehem. You will be traveling with me. The sooner we can get ready to go, the better it will be. It will take time to get things finished here. I won't take any more orders, but I have to complete the ones I already have. We have no idea how long we will be away, or even if it will be safe to return, so we must plan as though we are not coming back."

"But what will we tell people?" Mary asked worriedly.

"That my skill as a carpenter is growing, and I think I can do better for our family if we move to a larger town. Your parents are the only ones here who know you are carrying the Messiah. You can tell them."

The weeks sped by as Mary and Joseph prepared for their move. They agreed that they would take nothing with them but what they could carry. They sold or gave away all their household effects, reasoning that they would be able to replace them with no difficulty in Bethlehem.

Mary's pregnancy progressed. She felt her baby move; he was growing and taking up more space. She talked to him and sang to him as she rubbed her hand over her expanding abdomen. She spent as much time as she could spare walking and making herself ready for the long trip. It would not do for her to be a burden on the way to Bethlehem.

They decided they would leave Nazareth in early spring. The weather would be more favorable for travel. They would be able to sleep outside if necessary, and the sun would not be as intensely hot during the day. It was a month until she was due to give birth. Considering that the trip would take them about a week, they would have a couple of weeks to find a place to stay once they arrived in Bethlehem.

They had a few discussions, sometimes heated, about the wisdom or folly of spending their hard-earned money on a donkey. Mary insisted strongly that she was able to walk and carry her share of the load. Joseph insisted equally as strongly that they should be prepared in case the walk or the load was too much for her. When her father added his voice to Joseph's, Mary knew she had lost. Her determination to stay off the donkey's back increased with her capitulation.

The day of departure arrived. Mary knew Joseph was eager to begin, but her mother kept thinking of things she had to tell them, had to give them. Finally, with even Joseph's patience wearing thin, Anna looked him in the eyes, her own brimming with tears.

"Take good care of her. Bring her back safely to me when you can. Guard the baby. God go with you."

"I will, and He is, Mother," Joseph told her gently as he gave her one more hug.

Mary turned around as they made their way toward the road. Her mother had already gone inside her home. She had told Mary she didn't want to watch them leave.

"Here we go, baby," she whispered. "We're going to find you a home."

"What did you say?" Joseph asked.

"I was just talking to Jesus," she replied.

Joseph smiled and squeezed her hand.

For the first few days Joseph insisted on taking it easy. They had a lot of time, he reasoned. It wouldn't be smart to push too hard at the beginning and then lose time because of an accident or an injury.

There were always other travelers going in their direction, so they camped at night with groups large enough to provide safety. They were careful about what they told, but most people understood that when Caesar made a pronouncement, there was no question but to obey. It was required, it was expected, and it was done.

By the end of a week, Mary was getting very tired. It was growing increasingly difficult to make her legs move. Her left hip was giving her a great deal of pain, and it was impossible to hide it from Joseph, especially in the early morning. An added discomfort was her need to keep finding cover to relieve herself, as the growing child took more and more room.

Why couldn't I just have stayed home? she thought in despair. Immediately words from the prophet Micah came to her. *"But you, Bethlehem Ephrathah, though you are small among the clans of Judah, out of you will come for me one who will be ruler over Israel, whose origins are from of old, from ancient times."*

"God, forgive my weakness," Mary prayed in a murmur. "I know You are working things out in Your way, and I know that You will help me as I need it. Protect Your Son."

As they resumed the journey the next morning Mary was amazed at how much better she felt. Her hip had ceased complaining for the moment, and she could draw a full breath without being dug in the ribs by a sharp little heel or elbow.

"I feel like I could conquer the world today, Joseph!" she exclaimed.

"Don't say that too loud," he replied. "You don't know who might be listening."

Mary laughed. It was so good to be traveling with this man, her husband. She loved his seriousness, his sense of fun, his care and concern—everything about him.

"I think I'll start the day walking," she told him. "I feel like doing something. I need to get some more exercise. I couldn't sit still if I tried. I think I could walk halfway around the world today!"

"You don't need to go that far. We should reach Bethlehem today, if all goes well. Don't overdo it, please."

Mary assured Joseph she would be sensible, and they set off at an easy pace. By midday she was beginning to experience what she thought was cramping—just a slight tightening in her abdomen every little while. It wasn't terribly uncomfortable, so she said nothing to Joseph, lest he make her get back on the donkey.

Through the afternoon, the pressure increased, and she realized with mounting panic that she was beginning labor.

"Joseph, I think I need to ride for a while." She spoke

quietly, but she couldn't keep the edge out of her voice. "I think the baby is coming."

Joseph lifted Mary onto the donkey and walked beside it as Mary rode. His face was serious as he turned toward her. "We should be there before sunset. Can you make it?"

"I'll just have to. It isn't as bad as what Elisabeth went through, so I think I still have some time." She smiled to reassure him. *This is God's baby*, she told herself. He would provide something for them.

Joseph urged the donkey on as fast as he could. The sun slowly sank toward the western horizon. As it slipped out of sight they could see the buildings on the edge of the town.

Mary was unprepared for the bustle of activity in Bethlehem. People were coming and going, pushing, calling to each other, shouting over the noise and confusion. Joseph was struggling to keep the donkey moving ahead in the unfamiliar crowds of people. Mary's discomfort was growing. All she wanted now was a place to lie down. Involuntarily, her fists clenched in her lap until her knuckles turned white, but she didn't make any sound.

Joseph stopped at the first inn they came to.

"Do you have a place for two people to stay for the night?" he asked.

The innkeeper stared at Mary. He simply shook his head and turned his back on them.

Joseph stopped another traveler to ask directions. The traveler was helpful, but not hopeful. He had tried several places, but they couldn't accommodate him. Mary felt his eyes go over her, and he spoke quietly to Joseph. "Maybe if they see your wife, they'll be more sympathetic." He moved on.

At the door the traveler had pointed out to them, Joseph stopped. He entered, and Mary could hear an exchange of words.

Please hurry. Please hurry. Please hurry. The words went through her head like a prayer.

When Joseph emerged, he was not smiling. "They don't have any room either. He said if I wanted, I could have the stable."

Mary had no hesitation. "Did you tell him we would take it?"

"What choice did I have?"

"Thank you! How far is it?"

"Just around the corner here. He says it's clean and warm with the animals in there. Wouldn't you think that God's Son would deserve a palace, or at least a comfortable bed in a clean house?" His voice sounded bitter.

Mary laid her hand on his arm and squeezed gently. "This will be fine. God is watching out for us."

He helped her off the donkey, and they went in, to the back of the stable, where there was more room. The hay was fresh and clean. Joseph spread his cloak, placed some of their blankets over it, and helped her to lie down.

"This is the best I can do for you. I am so sorry."

"This is wonderful. We are sheltered, and we're alone and private. The bed is more comfortable than what I've had for a week. Don't feel sorry for me." She gasped as a pain worse than any of the previous ones hit her. She gripped his hand until it subsided.

"Should I go find somebody to help?" he asked.

"There's no time. Don't you dare leave me!"

It seemed like forever, but it was really only a short space of time until Mary pushed with all her remaining strength and delivered, perfect and whole, the Savior of the world. His first cry, gentle and soft, was a beautiful sound.

Nervous as he was, Joseph cut and tied the cord, wrapped the baby in a soft blanket, and handed Him to Mary. She immediately unwrapped Him so she could examine the tiny, perfectly formed body, then rewrapped Him and cuddled Him close, allowing Him to nurse.

She was so tired, yet so happy and so content. This baby was hers, a part of her forever. She would give her life for Him.

Joseph went to the well and then made a small fire to heat water. Between the two of them, they managed to clean the baby and wrap Him in some of the clothes Mary had prepared for Him. Then Mary cleaned herself, placed her baby in the manger at her head, and tried to get some rest.

As tired and spent as she was, she was too excited to sleep. She kept hearing the soft cry, seeing the wrinkled, red face and the downy dark hair.

In the quiet darkness, Mary heard someone approaching. Joseph moved to the front of the stable.

"It's just some shepherds," he whispered to Mary. "They don't look dangerous. Maybe they just want to find shelter."

The ones in the lead were pulling the others along. Their faces shone with joy. The oldest of the group introduced himself as Abraham.

"We saw an angel! Then there were more of them. They told us God had sent a baby, a Savior. The lights were so bright! It's night, but out there, it was like day!"

The youngest shepherd, Jacob, who was just a boy, interrupted Abraham. "The angel told us not to be afraid. It wasn't like anything I've ever seen before. There were so many of them!"

The others nodded their agreement, big smiles still on their faces.

"We had to come see for ourselves," added the one called Simon. "The angel said He would be in a manger."

Mary's eyes widened in wonder. God had prepared the stable for them and sent a herald to shepherds. Yes, this Savior would be for the common people like themselves. Joseph showed them to the stall where Mary was resting. Mary reached into the manger and pulled her son toward her. The men knelt at her feet in awe at the sight of the baby. Abraham reached out a hand and lightly touched the baby's head, then pulled his hand back quickly, as though the touch had been involuntary.

As quickly as they had come, they faded away into the night.

four

By the time morning came, Mary had managed a bit of sleep, but she was so very weary. She knew her baby would soon want to eat, so she forced herself to sit up, trying to move quietly without disturbing Joseph. He was sitting at the entrance of the stall with his back against the wall, sound asleep. She smiled.

There was a small charcoal fire burning in their heating pan. Close to the fire sat a waterpot. Mary managed to get to her feet before Joseph sat up, wide awake and alert. He took in the situation at a glance, realized there was no cause for alarm, and smiled at Mary.

"Is there anything I can get for you?" he asked.

"Yes, I'd like some water in a bowl or a pan so I can wash a bit before I feed Jesus," she replied.

She was clean and ready for Him when He woke up, demanding immediate attention. She cuddled Him close as she fed Him, running her hand softly over the fuzzy head, opening the tiny hand and allowing the fingers to wrap around hers. When He finished nursing, she cleaned Him and hugged Him close again. This time she kissed the top of His head, savoring the warm, milky scent of newborn baby.

By the time she grew tired enough to put Him back in the manger, Joseph was ready to face the world. He brought her some of the food they had left in their bag and informed her he was setting out to find a more permanent place for them to stay. He assured her he would let the innkeeper know she was still there, so he would keep an eye and ear open for her.

Within minutes, he was back.

"The innkeeper knows of a house we can have if we're interested. It's near here and in good condition. Do you want to see it first, or do you want me to decide?"

"You would know much better than I would if the house is in good condition. Just make sure there is a good water supply somewhere close and that the neighborhood will be safe for a family."

"What a wise little wife you are!" he exclaimed. He bent over and placed a kiss on the end of her nose, then turned and left.

As tired as she was, she didn't dare go to sleep while Joseph was away. God had entrusted her with His Son, and she was not going to allow anything or anybody to threaten Him. She fashioned a seat for herself from clean straw and blankets so that she would be comfortable when she next had to feed her baby. She looked around the stable, now that it was light. It was clean, as the innkeeper had said. There was only one other donkey besides theirs, but there was a cow and her calf. The calf was not more than a day or so old. Mary felt a kinship with the cow as she nuzzled her calf, pushing it to a standing position so it could nurse.

The whole south-facing side of the stable was open, and the warm sun was streaming in, showing the dust motes as they floated lazily down. There were cobwebs in the corners, with industrious spiders mending or building more webs. She was studying the intricacies of one web when a female voice called out, "May I come in?"

At the same instant, a graying head appeared around the corner of the stable. "I'm Hannah. My husband is the innkeeper. Your husband told us this morning you had a son. May I come see Him?"

"Good morning, Hannah. My name's Mary. Please come in." Mary led the way to the manger and pulled back the blanket to reveal the tiny form. One fist was clenched up by His cheek, and His mouth was moving as though He were sucking. His dark hair was still lying close to His head, but His face had lost some of its redness. His eyelashes lay across His cheeks like the finest silk.

"May I please hold Him?" Her voice was pleading.

Mary lifted Him carefully and handed Him to the woman. Hannah held Him expertly, clucking to Him and making soft cooing noises.

"I never had a baby of my own," she confessed apologetically, "but I looked after babies for wealthy women before I was married. I even helped at the birthing of some of them. Thomas didn't tell me that you were in labor. He just said a young couple was sleeping in the stable. If he had told me last night, I would have come to help. Did everything go all right?"

"Everything was fine," Mary assured her. "Joseph was a bit nervous, but he did very well. I really didn't need anyone else." She chuckled. "Joseph probably would have preferred it if you had been here."

Hannah smiled as she cuddled the baby. Her rough forefinger ever so gently traced along the soft cheek. Her eyes never left His face.

"He's straight from God, isn't He!" she exclaimed.

Mary wondered in a panic how she knew but then thought she was referring to the fact that He was a newborn baby. Her answer was quiet, but heartfelt. "Yes, He certainly is."

"I don't mean just because He's so new," Hannah persisted. "The shepherds who came to visit you last night stopped at the inn on their way back. They told us about the visit from the angels. He's our Messiah, isn't He?"

Mary was quiet.

"For all my life, since I was old enough to understand, I have been waiting for the Messiah," Hannah continued. "I know there are dangers if the wrong people find out. If He really is our Messiah, then God will protect Him, won't He?"

"You are right, Hannah," Mary answered. "I have been forgetting that."

She went on to tell Hannah about the first appearance of the angel, Joseph's dream, her visit to Elisabeth, and then the discovery that the baby was to be born in Bethlehem.

Hannah looked at her with tears in her eyes. "To think God chose us to help! I think we failed the test. If I had known, I would have given up my own room."

"Failed?" Mary asked. "You have no idea how warm and welcoming this stable was! The shepherds wouldn't have been as free to come if we were inside the inn. Your husband could have just told us he had no room at all. He didn't have to let us use the stable. God knows what He is doing."

Hannah held the baby until He woke up, needing to be fed. Then she reluctantly passed Him back to His mother.

"If you ever need someone to help with Him, please let me. The house your husband is looking at is just a very short distance away. I could be there very quickly."

"I promise you that if I ever need anyone, I will be very pleased to ask you. You don't need to wait for me to ask you, though. You can come to see us when you have time."

Joseph returned before Mary was finished feeding Jesus, and Hannah left them alone.

"The house is good," he told her. "It is large enough for a good-sized family, and there is a room I could use for a workshop, too."

"How far away is the well?"

"Within a stone's throw of the house."

"Yours or mine?" Mary asked with a smile.

Joseph studied her for a few seconds, then returned the smile. "Mine."

While she finished feeding and changing the baby, Joseph repacked their things on the donkey.

"Are you going to be able to walk that far carrying the baby?" he asked.

"I could get Hannah to carry him, and then I would just have to walk. You go ahead; Hannah knows the way."

"I'll stop and tell her you'd like her help. Thomas told me I could continue to stable the donkey here if I wished. He also told me where I could get the best bargains on the things we will need for my shop and for the house. They are so kind and helpful."

"God is looking after us."

Joseph nodded and went on his way. Hannah arrived so quickly, Mary suspected she had been just out of earshot.

When she was ready, Mary handed Jesus to Hannah, and they set out slowly. The house was on the outskirts of the town, with small bushes behind it. It was not near the main road into the town, so the road in front of the house would not be too noisy. Mary was pleased with Joseph's decision.

"I will be very happy here," she decided.

Joseph had unloaded the donkey and was ready to go to the marketplace to pick up the things they would need to set up housekeeping. Hannah informed him that she would stay with Mary until he returned.

"It's not that I think you really need me," Hannah explained after Joseph had left. "It is just that you are a stranger in a strange town, and I want to help. May I go get water for you?"

"I think I need you more than you know," Mary replied. "Yes, please. I could use some water." She sat on the pile of blankets and clothing Joseph had left against the wall, holding her baby close until Hannah returned.

Through the rest of the day, Joseph came and went, bringing loads of things they needed and replenishing his wood supply for the shop. Hannah stayed close, putting things away under Mary's direction, helping her to set up the bed and then insisting that she lie down for a rest. By the time the sun had set, the household was well established, even to a simple supper Hannah had left cooking over the fire.

When the baby was eight days old, Joseph circumcised Him and officially gave Him the name of Jesus. Hannah and Thomas were present to celebrate with them. Hannah had spent a part of each day with them, telling them she was making sure Mary was not doing more than she thought was good for her. Mary suspected it was because she wanted to be with Jesus as much as she possibly could. Mary did appreciate the extra pair of hands that was always willing to do whatever task was needed, whether it was helping with laundry, going for water, preparing a meal or looking after Jesus. She fought a brief battle with herself over the time that Hannah spent with her baby, but her compassionate heart won the battle. Jesus would always be her son. If they had to move, He would be going with them. Hannah would be left behind. Hannah could not feed Him, so Mary was able to hold Him at feeding times even when Hannah was present. Hannah would never have a child; Mary was young and had already had one child with no problem. There was no reason to think that Jesus would be her only child.

When Jesus was about six weeks old, it was time for Joseph and Mary to present Mary's purification offering at the temple in Jerusalem. At the same time they made plans to take Jesus to present Him to the Lord. Very early in the morning, before it was fully light, they set out. This time Mary didn't complain about riding on the donkey. She rode as long as she was comfortable, holding her baby close, talking to Him, soaking up the time she could spend with Him without having to think about the household chores that needed to be done. When she was too uncomfortable to ride any farther, Joseph carried Jesus while Mary led the donkey. Mary enjoyed watching Joseph with Jesus. He was already telling Him the things they had been taught about the Messiah, reciting from the books of Moses and telling him about the world they lived in. When Jesus was awake, His eyes were fixed on Joseph as he talked. Some of the time He stared as though He understood every word, some of the time He smiled, and then He yawned and fell asleep in the middle of an oration.

As they approached the temple, Joseph began singing some of the songs of ascents. They purchased a pair of turtledoves for the sin offering and presented themselves before the priest.

As they made their way to the outer court, an old man stopped them. "May I hold your child?" he asked.

Mary looked at Joseph, then passed Jesus to the man. Immediately he began praying, holding the baby reverently.

"Sovereign Lord, as you have promised, you now dismiss your servant in peace. For my eyes have seen your salvation, which you have prepared in the sight of all people, a light for revelation to the Gentiles and for glory to your people Israel."

Then he gave Joseph and Mary a special blessing. Turning to Mary, he said, "This child is destined to cause the falling and rising of many in Israel, and to be a sign that will be spoken against, so that the thoughts of many hearts will be revealed. And a sword will pierce your own soul too." He handed the baby back to her and silently went on his way.

Mary held Jesus closely, wishing she had not heard his last words. Her thoughts churned. *Why will a sword pierce my soul? He is going to be our Messiah, our deliverer, and our king. He will be victorious!*

Before she was able to fathom the meaning of his words, they were stopped again, this time by an elderly woman. She spoke to them about their special son, praising God for Him; then, turning to a couple who stood nearby, she told them that this was the Messiah, the hope for the redemption of Jerusalem.

Mary and Joseph were alarmed, but she turned back to them, laying her hand on Mary's arm.

"Don't be afraid. God has shown me those who are looking forward to deliverance. He will not allow harm to come to His chosen one before the time."

Mary and Joseph made their way silently out of the temple courtyard and headed for Bethlehem. They were both beyond tired but wanted to get to the safety of their home. They traveled in silence for a time, thinking about the things they had heard.

Joseph finally broke the silence. "This has been a strange day. Is God going to keep surprising us all the way through?"

Mary thought long before she spoke. "Maybe, until we become used to the idea that this is His child, He will have to keep reminding us."

They estimated that they would arrive back home before sunset. Jesus was beginning to be restless, needing to be changed and fed, so they stopped again just outside Bethlehem.

"I know we could probably get home before you feed Him, but why should He suffer when there is no real need?"

Joseph's comment stayed with Mary for many years.

It was just a few minutes past sunset when they finally got home. Joseph offered to go fetch water while Mary built up the fire for their meal. When they walked inside, Mary exclaimed, "Hannah!"

The fire was built up, the supper was prepared, and two full waterpots stood beside the door, a warm testimony of the caring of the older woman.

The days settled into a routine for Mary. She found she no longer had to fetch the water. There were always full waterpots sitting by the door. Joseph would fill the empty jars before he went to bed, and then if they needed refilling the next day, Hannah would go, usually when Mary was feeding Jesus. She was busy but very happy, and her marriage was thriving.

Things continued in a predictable pattern. Jesus grew and developed, delighting Joseph and Mary with His accomplishments. He smiled and tried to respond when they talked to Him. Joseph's carpentry business was becoming lucrative as his reputation for excellence and attention to detail became known.

One day when Jesus was six months old, visitors arrived at their home after their evening meal. At first Mary thought they wanted Joseph to build something for them. As she studied their facial features and their manner of dress, she realized they had come from a great distance. They spoke slowly and carefully, as if they weren't sure of the correct words to use, as if they were not familiar with the language. Joseph asked them to come in, and Mary hurriedly prepared a meal for them.

One of them was the spokesman for the rest. "We come far, long time." He used his hands to indicate that they had come from the east. "You have special child, king."

Mary and Joseph exchanged quick, alarmed glances. Things had seemed so normal that Mary had almost forgotten that Jesus was God's son. She picked Jesus up from His bed in the corner of the room, where He had been sleeping quietly. Her eyes didn't leave His face as He slowly began to wake up, disturbed from His rest.

A movement caught her eye, and she looked up to see the men kneeling before her, offering gifts, precious gifts, to her son. They opened an ornate chest they had with them, and she could see gold coins in it. The aroma of incense filled the room, and a beautifully decorated bottle held an expensive perfume. These they lay before Jesus. The tiny child waved His hands and watched them as they bowed low and then sat back on their heels to look at their king.

Mary watched their eyes as they continued their worship in their own language. She knew they presented no threat to either Joseph, herself, or Jesus, yet she still felt a chill of apprehension, as though things were about to change again.

As they rose to their feet, Jesus smiled at them, making delighted little baby noises, waving His tiny chubby hands. The man who had been the spokesman stepped forward, took one of the tiny hands in his own and pressed a kiss on the palm. Then they all turned and left without another word, leaving their gifts as the only evidence that they had even been in the house.

"Why, Joseph?" Mary asked quietly after all sound of them had receded. "You are doing well. Why do we need all this?"

"God will show us in His time."

Neither of them slept well that night. Mary lay awake, staring into the darkness, trying to calm her thoughts. She could feel Joseph tossing beside her. Then he sat up so abruptly, it startled her.

"What is it?" she asked.

"We have to leave. We have to go to Egypt. Now."

Joseph was on his feet fumbling for the lamp, lighting it from the dying embers of the fire. "Pack up what you can. We have to leave as soon as we can get away. We must be out of Bethlehem before the sun comes up."

"What about Hannah?" Mary asked. "Can I leave her a message?"

"We can't tell anyone anything. If they don't know, they can't be forced to tell."

They rushed around, packing all they could. Joseph slipped out to the stable and brought back the donkey that had served them so well. He loaded as much on its back as he could, making sure that Mary and Jesus would still be comfortable if they needed to ride. Then he tied pieces of an old robe around its hooves. Mary knew then that he believed they were in terrible danger. There were some things they couldn't take with them, and Mary hoped that Hannah would be able to make use of them.

"O God, somehow, could you let her know why we had to go?" Mary prayed.

Joseph took her by the shoulders and looked into her face. His face was drawn as if he were in great pain. "She will know. She will know."

They left quickly and quietly, keeping to the smaller, narrower streets until they reached the southern outskirts of the city. They traveled steadily until the dawn began to lighten the sky toward the east. Joseph allowed Mary to take a brief rest and feed Jesus before they continued on as swiftly as they could go.

For several more hours they pushed on, until they were so tired they were stumbling. They stopped at the inn in Hebron, giving the donkey a chance to rest while they caught up on some lost sleep. By mutual consent, they avoided other travelers, lest they be asked questions they didn't want to answer.

Joseph went alone to the market to buy food for the rest of their journey. As sundown approached, they were ready to push onward.

"The next town will be Beersheba, so we have quite a journey ahead of us. I don't think we can do it without stopping along the way for sleep," Joseph informed her after they were outside the town.

"We were in such a rush last night that I didn't even ask you why we are going to Egypt. Did God tell you?"

"I had another dream. It was so vivid, like when the angel told me to take you as my wife. Only this time he warned me to get out of Bethlehem as soon as possible. Those men had come from Jerusalem. They must have talked to Herod. The angel told me Herod was going to try to kill Jesus."

"Why? He's only a baby!" Mary cuddled Him closer.

"If they told him they were looking for a king, he would want to get rid of Him, no matter how little He is."

"But he wouldn't know where to look," Mary replied. "How would he know which baby was the right one?"

"He wouldn't know. So he would have to make sure, wouldn't he?"

As realization dawned, Mary felt as if she couldn't bear the horror of what was to come in Bethlehem. "Isn't there anything we can do?" she pleaded. "We must be able to do something!"

"We are doing what God has told us to do. That is all we *can* do." Joseph's voice sounded harsh.

"But, Joseph—"

"We have to be obedient." Joseph interrupted. "If we were to disobey and go back, Jesus could be killed before He becomes king. That wouldn't accomplish anything."

"But I feel so helpless and almost guilty that Jesus is safe when all those other babies are in danger," Mary persisted.

"We have to trust that God will take care of the other details in His way and in His own time," Joseph said. "Do you remember what you said to the angel when he told you God had chosen you to bear the Messiah?"

"I will do as the Lord has required. May His will be done." Mary spoke in a whisper. "Yes, Joseph, He knows what is best."

They both walked in silence for a long time. Mary's thoughts churned. She was fighting anger, fear, and an overwhelming anguish. Tears ran down her cheeks as she tried to form the words for prayer. Finally she gave up searching for the words and just turned her emotions over to God.

An incredible peace flooded through her, and she became aware of God's presence in a way she never had before. She felt strength and energy pouring into her and a love, indescribable, enveloping her. She knew that God understood what she was feeling. She knew that He, the Creator of all life, would be as sad as she was over the deaths of so many innocent babies. She knew He would feel the anguish of the families that would be affected. He did not condemn her for her anger and grief; He shared it with her.

She began singing softly. "Let everyone who is godly pray to you while you may be found; surely when the mighty waters rise, they will not reach him. You are my hiding place; you will protect me from trouble and surround me with songs of deliverance."

Joseph placed a strong, comforting hand on her shoulder and quoted quietly, "The eternal God is your refuge, and underneath are the everlasting arms."

five

EACH MORNING OF THE JOURNEY MARY AWOKE TO THE SAME scenery—desert sand, broken only by short scrubby brown vegetation. One afternoon, she saw shimmering in the distance.

"Joseph! Am I seeing things? That looks like water!"

Joseph questioned others who were more familiar with the route, then came back to Mary.

"That's the Great Sea. It *is* water, but it's salty."

"The Great Sea?" Mary stared in awe. As they drew closer, her wonderment grew. Water stretched endlessly to the horizon and beyond, as far as they could see.

As long as they could they traveled along the coast, where a bit of a breeze gave relief from the heat of the desert sun. Mary held Jesus up so He could see the water.

"My dear little son, do you see this? This is the Great Sea! I have never seen so much water in all my life! Can you believe it?"

Jesus smiled at his mother but didn't share her interest in the vastness of the sea.

Joseph laughed. "Mary, do you realize He was present when all of this was created? Of course He believes it."

The love in his voice let her know he was not being critical, just bringing her back to the realization that her son was God in the flesh.

After traveling for three weeks following the caravan route from Beersheba, they arrived in Egypt. They rested for a few hours at an inn before Joseph set out to find them a permanent place to live. Mary cuddled Jesus close as He slept peacefully, unaware of the bustle around Him.

Mary found it so much busier than Bethlehem had been. It was the first trading center since they had left Beersheba, and a caravan arrived just after Joseph left. Mary watched the traders covertly, not wanting to be noticed as being a foreigner. She heard many languages she didn't know, but then her ears detected a familiar dialect. She had heard it used in the marketplace in Bethlehem. She listened intently with her eyes cast down.

"Herod ordered that they all be killed."

"Why?"

"He was trying to get rid of a possible rival."

"A rival? How could a child be a rival?"

"They said he heard a rumor that a king had been born in Bethlehem. He didn't know where or when, so he ordered that all the boys under the age of two be killed. They were."

"How do you know?"

"We came through there the day after they finished. It was a terrible place to be. I don't envy that man when he meets his God."

Mary's breath caught, and she gasped before she could stop herself. The two men turned toward her. Her eyes filled with tears as she returned their nodded greetings. The younger of the two men came closer to her.

"Did you come from there?" he asked.

Mary nodded.

"Lucky escape for your little one, then."

The older man approached. "That's not luck. God was looking after this one."

Mary smiled through her tears.

The man knelt down so he could see the sleeping face of the baby. He spoke so softly that only Mary could hear him. "God must have a special job for this little one to do to take Him out of that. I'll never forget it." He shook his graying head, and tears came into his own eyes.

Mary reached out her hand and laid it on his arm. The abrupt movement awakened Jesus, and He sat up to look at the man who was so close. His big brown eyes stared unblinkingly into the bearded older face. Suddenly, His face lit up with a smile, and His little hands waved in the air. He crowed as the man returned his smile.

The younger man had moved away, quickly losing interest in a mother with a baby. The older man continued speaking softly. "He's the one Herod was looking for, isn't He? He is our king, our Messiah."

"What would make you say that?" asked Mary. Her heart was pounding, and she was praying desperately for God's protection.

"I have been looking for our Messiah for a long, long time, and now I have such a peace, as if I have no need to look any more. My name is Benjamin. I come through Egypt a couple of times a year. If you are going to be here long, I'd like to visit when I'm back, if I may."

"We will be here until God tells us to leave," she answered.

Over the man's shoulder she saw Joseph approaching. "Here's my husband now. He may be able to tell you more."

Benjamin turned and introduced himself to Joseph. He placed his strong hand on Joseph's shoulder and very quietly let him know he was a seeker of the Messiah.

Joseph took his hand with a smile, not giving anything away, but not closing the door on a possible ally. "It is good to find a fellow seeker."

Benjamin persisted. "I know I have found Him in this child. I would do nothing to bring harm to Him, or to you and His mother."

Joseph embraced the man, then turned to Mary. "I've found a home that will do us for now. Do you want to come now or wait until later?"

Mary stood up. "I'm ready to come now. Joseph?" She nodded toward Benjamin.

Joseph picked up on her cue. "Benjamin, would you like to accompany us to our new home? What we have is simple, but you are welcome to share it with us."

Benjamin agreed readily and helped as Joseph led the donkey through the busy streets.

"This area is where our forefathers lived when they were in Egypt," he told them. "This is the land of Goshen. It has changed a bit since they lived here, but think of walking on the same ground as Moses and Aaron!"

Mary's mind immediately centered on Moses' mother, on the things she had done to save her son, and how he had become a deliverer for his people. She looked down at the soft little bundle in her arms, wondering if she would be willing to give Him to someone else to save His life. *Yes,* she decided. *I would do whatever it took to save His life.* She was extremely thankful that she had not been called on to do that yet.

If God asks me to give Him up, He will also give me the strength to bear it, she decided. By the time she had the matter settled in her mind, Joseph had led them to their new home. It was smaller than the one they had left in Bethlehem but certainly adequate for their needs at the present time. There was only one room for their living space and one room for Joseph's workshop.

"I don't think we will be here for very long, certainly not more than a year," explained Joseph apologetically.

Mary smiled at him. "This is all we need until God shows us the next step."

Again they began the task of setting up their home, but this time without the willing hands of Hannah. Benjamin stayed with them for a few days until his caravan was ready to move on. While Mary did appreciate his help, she greatly missed the friendship she had shared with Hannah. On his last morning with them, she asked when he would be going through Bethlehem again and if he could deliver a message to Hannah for her.

"Just tell her that you have seen us, that we are safe and settling in, and that God is still watching over His chosen one." Then she added, with a smile, "And when we come back, we will stop to see her."

"I will do even better than that," he replied. "When I come back, I will bring you news of her."

"Do you ever go through Nazareth?" she asked.

"Yes, on our way to Damascus we make a stop in Nazareth. What can I do for you there?"

"Ask for Joses and Anna. They're my parents. Tell them the baby is seven months old and doing well. Don't tell them where we are. Let them know we're no longer in Bethlehem, but we're in God's care, healthy and content, and we think of them often."

"I would be very pleased to deliver that message to them. If there's a return message, I will bring it when I come back."

Mary's heart overflowed with joy and gladness as the realization hit her that this was another special person God had placed into their lives for care and comfort.

"Before a word is on my tongue you know it completely, O LORD. You hem me in—behind and before; you have laid your hand upon me. Such knowledge is too wonderful for me, too lofty for me to attain."

She looked apologetically at Benjamin. "Whenever God overwhelms me with His love and care, I just have to sing about it."

Benjamin placed his hand on her head. "I know why He has chosen you as the mother of the Messiah. You have such a joyful faith in Him. Don't ever change!" He turned to Joseph, grasping his hand warmly. "May God always guide and protect your family. If He so wills, I will return in a few months' time." Then he was gone.

six

JOSEPH SET UP HIS WORKSHOP IMMEDIATELY AND BEGAN preparing items of furniture to sell. In a matter of days he had customers placing orders for simple articles. As time went on, he became busier, and orders came in for more complicated pieces.

Mary busied herself with the household chores, finding it more difficult to accomplish the work without Hannah's help. One morning, Jesus was fussing, wanting to be held. Mary stopped in the midst of her meal preparation to cuddle the baby, nursing Him briefly.

"Did Hannah spoil me, God?" she asked. "I just can't seem to get anything done. I know other mothers manage; why can't I?"

Very clearly the answer came back. "You decide what is most important. Is it your child or your house?"

The midday meal was a bit late, but she offered no apologies, and none were required. Joseph took the extra time to hold and talk to Jesus, entertaining Him while Mary finished the preparations.

That afternoon she found Jesus to be fretful and a bit feverish. Again she turned to God. "O God, He is Your Son, and He seems to be sick. What should I do? Show me."

By evening she was worn out with concern and with tending the little one. Joseph came back from the marketplace and immediately took over for her while she hurriedly prepared the evening meal.

"I think he's teething," Joseph observed, watching Jesus chew on His fists with increasing ferocity.

"Of course!" Mary replied. "Why didn't I think of that! Thank You, God, for my wise husband."

After they had eaten, Joseph went to his workshop for a short time, coming back with a perfectly smooth piece of wood for the baby to chew on. "I've been working on this for a few days in my spare time, knowing He would soon need it."

Mary was amazed at the simple device. It was circular in shape with a hollow center, like an oversized ring with rounded edges. It would be impossible for Him to get the whole thing in His mouth at a time, yet it was easy for Him to hold. It seemed to be what He wanted and needed, and her work was made a bit easier.

In time, the worst of the teething passed, and her baby was showing a more mature smile with the white teeth in evidence. Jesus began to crawl and explore and even pull Himself to His feet. Both Mary and Joseph watched His progress with awe, as all parents do, marveling at the new things He was learning every day.

Mary had formed a friendship of sorts with a few of the nearby women, but language was a barrier, and the religion and traditions were very different. She also thought that the fewer people she became close to, the easier it would be when the time came to leave. She still missed Hannah, though a few months had passed since they left Bethlehem.

Around this time, Mary suspected she might again be with child. Her energy was flagging, and the thought of food had begun to turn her stomach. She recognized some of the familiar signs but didn't want to say anything until she was sure. When Joseph caught her napping while her bread was baking, she decided it was time to pass along her news. His face broke into a broad smile, and he gave her a hug.

"I wonder where this baby will be born," she wondered aloud. In her heart, she wanted to be back home, with her mother close by. This child wasn't destined to be the Messiah, so God wouldn't be protecting and providing in quite the same way.

"Wherever God wills" was Joseph's answer.

Although she knew he was right, it annoyed her a bit that he seemed so matter of fact about it. She thought about the answer for a time and then gave her concern and worry to God.

"I know You know what is best for all of us. I know You love this little one. Just give me Your peace, and give me patience to wait for Your time."

As always, the peace came.

Over the next couple of months, her tiredness and nausea were replaced by an increasing appetite and level of energy. It was necessary. Her formerly helpless tiny baby had turned into a busy exploring toddler. He wasn't willful or disobedient; He was curious and needed to investigate His world.

According to Mary's calculations, the new baby was due to be born in about six months' time. She had been out walking, allowing Jesus to wander farther than usual on His sturdy little legs. She turned Him toward home again.

As she approached the door she noticed a large pack sitting on the doorstep. At first she felt relief. Joseph had said that morning that he was almost finished his last order, and no more had come in. She knew that God would provide as they needed it, but she also knew it would bother Joseph if he couldn't stay busy.

She heard voices coming from the workshop. She recognized Joseph's, but the identity of the other, although somewhat familiar, eluded her. Joseph heard Jesus' chatter as they entered and called for Mary to come through to the workshop.

"Benjamin!" she exclaimed, holding her arms out for a hug.

Benjamin hugged her, then turned and scooped up the toddler. Jesus studied him. Then He smiled and snuggled close.

"He's grown a lot, hasn't he?" Benjamin said. "He was just a babe in arms when I left, and now He's walking. How is He?"

Mary replied, "He is the best baby that ever was. He did give us a bit of trouble when He was cutting teeth, but He is such a good little boy!

"Have you been through Bethlehem again? Did you get as far as Damascus this time? Did you see any of my family, or Hannah?"

Benjamin and Joseph both laughed.

"Which question should I answer first?" Benjamin joked. "I can answer them all with one word: 'Yes.'"

"Will you stay and eat with us and tell us all your news?" asked Joseph.

Benjamin agreed to stay. Mary hurried with the meal preparation, helped by the fact that Benjamin insisted on looking after Jesus for her.

After they finished eating, Benjamin shared his messages.

"Hannah is well. She was very happy to hear that all of you are safe. She was afraid that something terrible had happened to you at first, but when Herod sent his soldiers, she knew God's protection was over you. Still, she was relieved. She sent a little gift for Jesus. She thought it would be some time before He could use them, but I think He could make good use of them now."

He turned to his pack and removed a small package. It was a tiny pair of sandals that Hannah had fashioned.

Mary's eyes filled with tears as she looked them over. She could picture the bent gray head of the older woman as she worked away at the special little gift. "Tell her I said thank you from the bottom of my heart."

"She also told me that she rescued your things before they could be confiscated. She is storing them in case you can use them later.

"Your parents aren't doing quite as well. Your father is ill, and your mother is tired from caring for him. She thinks he will soon be taken to his fathers. She was very pleased to hear of you. She knew God would be protecting you and the child. She would love to see you, but she said to tell you that you must be obedient to the voice of God."

It was late before they slept. There was so much to talk about! Benjamin told them that Herod was rumored to be dying. He was not seen in public any more, and the reports said that he could not even rise from his bed.

After they went to bed, Mary lay awake a long time, going over the news that Benjamin had brought. Then she turned to God in prayer. "I would like to see my father before he dies. I would like to help my mother with his care, but, God, I will not fuss. I will wait patiently for Your time. Help my mother to know that I am praying for her. Give her the strength she needs day by day."

Before dawn, Joseph awakened her. "I've had another dream. God has said it is safe for us to leave Egypt! Herod has died."

"Will we go back to Bethlehem?" asked Mary.

"No. He's calling us back to Nazareth."

"Thank You, God!" was Mary's reply.

At breakfast, they told Benjamin about God's message.

"When will you go?" he asked.

"As soon as we can get ready."

"The caravan is leaving in two days' time. You could travel with us as far as Bethlehem. It would give you safety and company and would give me someone to talk to as we travel."

"Would we be allowed?" asked Mary.

"The roads are free for anyone to travel. You would just be traveling at the same time we are. But to set your mind at rest, I will ask the leader."

Later that day Benjamin returned with the man himself, who had come to check out the family. Mary was surprised to see how much he resembled the men who had brought the gifts to Jesus while they were still in Bethlehem. He was very businesslike, but courteous. Through Benjamin, he greeted them and assured them that he would be pleased to have the family travel with the caravan. He offered the use of camels if they needed them, for a modest price. Joseph said they would keep it in mind, but they did have a donkey, if it wouldn't be too slow. The trader smiled when Benjamin translated the message. He told them that a donkey was much slower than the camels, and it might be better to sell the donkey in Egypt and buy a new one when they arrived in Bethlehem. He would be pleased to help Joseph find the right buyer in Egypt and then find the right donkey for them again in Bethlehem.

Joseph looked at Mary. She nodded slightly. The donkey had served them well, but he was getting older and was not able to travel at the pace that would be necessary. If they could find a good place for him where he would be treated well, they would not regret leaving him behind.

Joseph asked Benjamin to convey his gratitude to the trader. He would try to find a buyer that day, and if he was not successful, he would ask for the trader's help. The man bowed low and departed silently.

Benjamin and Joseph set out immediately to a few customers Joseph had in mind who would be able to use the donkey and also would be kind to him. Within a short time they were back. They had found a family who had need of a donkey. They were able to pay the price Joseph asked, and they were known to be very kind to the animals in their care.

The evening was a busy one as Joseph and Mary sorted through their belongings and decided what could be left behind and what would have to travel with them.

In the midst of their packing, Mary stopped suddenly and exclaimed, "I was concerned that you had no new orders. God knew we would be leaving, and He was preparing the way for us. He is so good!"

By the next afternoon, they were ready. Benjamin departed and returned with a camel, ready for loading.

Mary laughed at how tiny the bundle seemed on the huge beast. "That would have covered the poor little donkey, and he still has room for a rider!"

Early in the evening they set out. Riding the camel took more energy than riding the donkey, but Benjamin promised Mary that she would soon become accustomed to the motion and be able to relax. Jesus had no problem. As soon as they began, He was lulled to sleep by the rocking motion. Mary tried to relax, but it was such a long way to the ground, and she was certain she would be trampled by those huge feet if she were to take a tumble. Benjamin rode beside her for a while until she felt more confident. Then he dropped back to ride beside Joseph.

Before Mary realized it, the motion and the low sounds of the voices around her had put her to sleep as well. She rested securely in the seat that had been fashioned especially for riders. When she awoke, they had already covered many miles, and they were giving the camels a break. Dawn was beginning to lighten the sky in the east as they stopped. She took the opportunity to feed Jesus a bit of food while they were still, then let Him run for a bit of exercise. She realized that He was the center of everyone's attention, being the youngest member of the caravan. Many of the older men made a point of coming to see the little one and talk to Him. He watched each face without fear and with great interest, almost, Mary thought, as though He could understand the words they were speaking.

Mary and Joseph were both amazed at the distance they were able to travel in a day by camel. They knew they would be in Bethlehem in ten or eleven days.

seven

AT THE END OF TEN DAYS, MARY, ALTHOUGH BECOMING accustomed to riding the camel, was very tired of travel. Jesus was becoming more restless from the forced inactivity. The brief rests for the camels during the day were not enough to give active little legs the exercise they needed. Both Joseph and Benjamin took turns relieving Mary when she began to tire.

The journey ended just in time, as far as Mary was concerned. They would stop in Bethlehem for a few days to give everyone a chance to rest and to wait for another caravan to arrive from farther east. Mary and Joseph were told that if the other caravan arrived when it was expected, their caravan would not have to go down toward Sinai but would be able to go on to Damascus, and the leader would be more than willing for them to go with his group as far as they wanted.

Benjamin smiled as he relayed the trader's words. "He says he has never had such a smooth trip. He is sure you bring him good fortune. He even said he would not charge you anything from here to wherever you are going."

Mary was torn. A part of her wanted to stay longer in Bethlehem, visiting with Hannah and catching up on all that had happened there and in Goshen, but another part of her wanted to get home as quickly as possible to see her father and help her mother.

Her reunion with Hannah was joyful. They had so much to talk about, they kept interrupting each other; then they would both stop talking and laugh. It was so very good to be together again.

Almost immediately Mary told her when they would be leaving for Nazareth, so there would be no surprises. Although Hannah, too, was disappointed at the brief visit, they both agreed it was better than not seeing each other at all.

"Perhaps we will see each other at the special feast days in Jerusalem," Mary suggested.

"Or maybe I can persuade Thomas to move to Nazareth," whispered Hannah.

They laughed, knowing how well established Thomas's inn was in Bethlehem and how much Thomas and Hannah loved the people and the town, David's town.

In less than a week they were on their way again, this time on the last leg of a journey that had begun over a year before. They were even able to take the household effects Hannah had saved for them when they had fled into Egypt. Because they were traveling with a caravan, they went straight through Samaria and cut many miles from their trip.

In four days they were approaching Nazareth. Mary forced herself to remain calm and stay on the camel, realizing even through her impatience that she could not run as fast as the camel could walk.

Benjamin accompanied them with the camels to her parents' house, where they were greeted by a curious and then jubilant Anna. Mary hugged her mother fiercely, as though trying to make up for the long time they had been away.

Anna turned to Benjamin. "I give you a message; you bring me my daughter! I call that a good exchange." She kissed him on both cheeks.

"Mother," said Mary, "this is Jesus." She led the toddler by the hand to Anna, watching the two of them.

Anna knelt down with her arms open, and Jesus walked right between them for the hug that was coming. Tears ran down Anna's cheeks.

"I don't know whether to call You 'grandson' or 'Messiah.' Either way, You are a beautiful little one, and I love You."

Jesus reached up with a chubby hand and touched the older woman on the cheek, then nestled against her contentedly.

The next few days were a blur to Mary. There was so much to talk about, so much to catch up on, so much to do, so many places to be. By the end of the week they had found a home a short distance from her parents' house. It was far enough away to afford privacy, yet close enough that she could quickly give help to her mother as it was needed.

Her father was not always aware of what was going on around him. She found that difficult to deal with, since he had been her strong protector while she was growing up. He had been her fixer of everything, from broken toys to bruised knees.

Her daily routine included her own housework, looking after a busy little boy, and lending a hand and a listening ear to her mother. Often her mother would take Jesus out to give them both some exercise and a change of scenery. During the times Mary spent alone with her father, she told him of the things they had done and seen during the time they were away. She described the home in Egypt, in Goshen, where their ancestors had lived so long ago. She described the stable in Bethlehem where Jesus had been born. She told him of the gifts of friendship God had provided in Hannah and then in Benjamin. She told him about the visit from the shepherds, from the men of the east, from the angel. She told him how, even now, God was preparing people for the Messiah. How He let them know that Jesus was the chosen one. She told him about the times when God had given her peace and surrounded her with love like nothing she had ever before experienced.

One day as she spoke softly to him, he opened his eyes and looked directly at her. "Mary, my daughter. You have been greatly blessed by God. He has chosen you to be the mother of the king. To think that God has allowed me to see the means of deliverance for our people!" He closed his eyes again and slept. During the night he died.

As Mary and Anna prepared his body for burial, Mary brought out the anointing oil that the men from the east had given to them. "I think it would be fitting to use some of the oil for his burial. His last words were about our deliverer."

"But Mary, it's for Jesus," her mother protested.

"God understands. We will use just a small amount in his hair and his beard."

Her mother conceded, and together they anointed Joses for his burial.

For the week following the funeral, Mary stayed with her mother so Joseph and Jesus would not become unclean from their association with her. When the ritual cleansing was complete, she went back home. She had missed her little family more than she thought she would. The break had been good for her, helping her to realize how precious they were to her, helping her to be more patient with them as the time of her confinement drew nearer.

After the death of her father, they took her mother to live with them. So, as Mary had hoped, her mother was present for the birth of her second son, whom they named Joses, after his grandfather and *his* father. It was not a difficult birth, and she was more relaxed, knowing that she had accomplished it before. She found it so good to be able to lie back and let someone else take over everything. Her mother's helping hands were much appreciated in the days that followed as well. She allowed Mary the time to rest as she needed, looking after the meals, the household chores, and Jesus, her pride and joy.

At first Joseph protested that Anna was doing too much, but Mary assured him that her mother was happiest when she was busy and that she had the wisdom to know when she was doing too much.

eight

By the time Jesus was three and Joses was a year old, Mary knew she was again with child. Even with her mother's help, she found she didn't have time to feel tired or sick. There was always mending to do on the small garments, always food to prepare for the growing appetites, always little boys to keep an eye on and their questions to answer. She was very busy, but she was content and happy with her loved ones around her.

Joseph was a wonderfully patient and kind father, taking Jesus into the shop and helping Him make little toys and gifts for His younger brother, mother and grandmother. Mary knew that as each son came along, Joseph would do the same thing, preparing them to take over the work when he was no longer able and to provide for their own families when the time came.

One morning, just after Joseph had begun his work in the carpenter shop, they heard a commotion outside in the street. Immediately Mary sought her sons, who were both safely inside. They could hear bells jingling and neighborhood children shouting. As the sounds came closer, Joseph came in from the carpenter shop and scooped up Jesus before heading outside with a smile on his face. Anna picked up Joses and followed. Mary followed more slowly, as her increasing size would not allow her to move swiftly.

They could see two camels approaching the house, with a parade of children behind them. Camels didn't often pass through their neighborhood.

Immediately Mary's mind jumped to Benjamin, so she asked Joseph, "Could it be Benjamin?"

"It could be, and I'm assuming it is," Joseph's replied. "In the market a few days ago there were rumors of a caravan approaching, with the same leader who led our caravan when we came home."

"Why didn't you tell me sooner?" Mary asked. "I could have prepared something special for Benjamin!"

The wise Joseph smiled at his wife before he replied. "That is *exactly* why. I wasn't sure if Benjamin would still be in the caravan, and I didn't want you to be disappointed if he didn't come."

In spite of her annoyance with Joseph, Mary had to smile at him. This husband of hers knew her so well!

By now the camels had arrived, and not only Benjamin but the caravan leader as well dismounted from the camels.

Benjamin greeted Joseph, Jesus, Mary, and Anna. Then he touched Joses on the head and said, "So you were the little one we carried without seeing."

He introduced the caravan leader to Anna before he explained the reason for the visit. "My master, Esmail, promises he will not impose on your hospitality for long. He just wished to see that his best passengers were still doing well."

Mary smiled at the leader and said, "Benjamin, please tell this man we are very thankful for his help and his protection as we traveled. We are so much more in his debt than he ever could be in ours! Ask him if he will please stay and share a meal with us, as simple as it may be."

Benjamin translated the message, and Esmail laughed and then replied.

"He says he will be happy to stay, if you will accept a gift from him."

Mary looked at Joseph, and he nodded his consent.

Esmail turned to his camel and removed a large basket, then passed it to Benjamin. With Joseph's permission, Benjamin carry it into the house.

Mary and her mother were surprised and delighted to find large quantities of fresh and dried figs and dates, fresh pomegranates, and round dark-yellow-orange fruit with which they were unfamiliar.

"Benjamin, what are these?" Mary asked. "How do I prepare them? Or can we eat them as they are?"

"They're called 'narangahs.' You remove the outer layer, and you can eat them mixed with the dried figs and dates. They are a bit sour unless you sweeten them with fruit or honey."

Mary turned to Anna. "Mother, if you will prepare the bread for our meal, I will try to make a dish of fruit using the things Benjamin and Esmail have brought."

The two women worked together swiftly and soon had the not-so-simple meal ready for their guests.

The meal itself was an interesting one, as Joseph and Mary had questions for Benjamin and Esmail about their travels. Benjamin would translate the question, then wait for Esmail's answer before translating for Joseph, Mary, and Anna. He then would add his own opinions to what Esmail had shared.

Following the meal, Esmail took the two camels and returned to the rest of the caravan while Benjamin remained with them for the night. After the little ones were asleep, their talk turned to the political situation in the country and the difficulties that were arising in traveling from place to place. Benjamin also shared with them that Esmail was asking a lot of questions about what he called "Benjamin's God."

"I believe he is truly seeking the truth. He saw how different you were, how you treated him and how you treat each other. He has already mentioned that he likes the way I am with customers, treating them with respect—because they are people, not because they are wealthy. I have been able to share with him what our law says and how we are supposed to live. He's fascinated by the story of God leading us out of slavery in Egypt and making us into a nation."

Before they settled down to sleep, Joseph promised they would continue to pray for both Benjamin and Esmail.

Early in the morning Benjamin left, with a promise to return when he came through Nazareth again.

Mary thought of him and Esmail and prayed for them every time she prepared the fruit they had brought. She said to Anna, "I think I could eat all these narangahs by myself. They're so good, and so full of juice! What will I do when they're all gone?"

Anna laughed. "In a few months' time, you won't be as hungry for them. They taste extra good to you right now because you are with child."

A few months later, as Mary and Joseph were settling down for the night, Mary was surprised by a sharp pain in her abdomen. She gasped as the pain increased. By the time she could let Joseph know what was happening, Mary felt a gush. Then the familiar contractions began.

"Anna, you're needed!" he called, quietly but urgently.

Within an hour or two, Mary was holding her baby, her first daughter. "Our own little Hannah. Oh, Mother, she's so beautiful!" Her finger traced the shape of Hannah's dainty little face, still red and a bit wrinkled. "Just look at all the hair she has!"

Joseph was entranced by his daughter. "It's a good thing you have older brothers!" he exclaimed. "There's no way I could battle off the suitors by myself when you get old enough for them to notice you."

From the very beginning, Hannah's brothers were wonderful protectors, although Joses was not always wise in the ways he protected his little sister. Mary, Joseph, and Anna often found his toys next to her as she slept. After they discovered him trying to feed her a piece of bread, they had to be vigilant lest he try to feed her something else when she was hungry.

Mary tried to reason with the little boy. "Joses, I know you love your sister, but Mother is the only one who can feed Hannah while she is so little. She doesn't have teeth like you do, and her little tummy doesn't like the food that you eat." Joses was not happy that his care for his baby sister was unappreciated.

In a few months' time, Joseph started taking Joses with him to the carpenter shop, which provided an outlet for the busy toddler. Hannah was also getting old enough to let the grownups know when things were not to her liking.

Before Hannah was six months old Mary realized that she was again carrying new life. Although she would have preferred a bit more of a gap between her babies, she knew they would welcome this child with overflowing love. God had blessed them with so much, and His blessings included their children.

Just a few weeks after Hannah's first birthday, Mary gave birth to a very small boy. She knew he had not been in the womb long enough to give him a good start in the world. He and they fought bravely, but their tiny Simon wasn't strong enough for the fight and was taken from them before he was even a week old.

As Mary held the body of her little son, words from the Scriptures came to her mind: "*The LORD gave and the LORD has taken away; may the name of the LORD be praised.*"

Within a year, Mary gave birth to another little boy. This time the baby was strong and healthy, with a voice to rival his older brothers. Joseph and Mary named him James. A year later Rebekah joined the family, followed by Judah about eighteen months after that.

By this time, both Jesus and Joses were in the village school during the day. Hannah was beginning to be a helper, as Mary and Anna instructed her in looking after their home. She was still too little to fetch the water or make the fire, but she helped with sewing and food preparation. She was also a good helper with the babies, keeping them entertained if Mary and Anna were too busy to look after them.

As Anna grew older, she became more willing to take on the sedentary tasks of sewing and holding the little ones. "Having the time to hold a child is the special reward for growing old," she laughingly told Mary. "I don't have the energy to do all I used to do, but I will always have the energy to hold a baby."

Mary hugged her. "I have relied on your hands and your feet and your eyes almost all my life. Now I'm relying on your lap and your arms. I appreciate you more than I could ever tell you. Just to have you here with us is such a big blessing, not just to me but to Joseph and the children as well."

Just before Judah's second birthday, Mary and Joseph's last child was born. During Mary's pregnancy they had received word that her cousin Elisabeth had died. Their new baby was a girl, and they named her Elisabeth. Mary often wondered how Zachariah and ten-year-old John were doing without their Elisabeth.

As Jesus approached His twelfth birthday, Joseph told Mary that they would have to take Him to Jerusalem for the next Feast of the Passover. He was old enough.

Anna was now unable to make the journey, so she said she

would stay with the younger children, who were becoming old enough to be responsible around the home.

Joses taunted Jesus about going with the group that would depart for Jerusalem. "Just like one of the big men. You think You're so special! Wait until You get there. You'll be scared of all the crowds!"

Jesus looked at him silently for a few seconds before He answered, "A part of Me is scared already, but it's time for Me to go. Next year when it's your turn to go for the first time, I will be able to tell you what to expect, if you want Me to."

Mary watched as Joses rushed out of the house and disappeared. She sighed. "Why does he always take offense? Why does he always try to cause trouble?"

Joseph rested his hand on her shoulder. "It's difficult for Joses to be the younger brother to someone so wise and loving, who never picks on the younger ones, who is always ready with a kind word and a helping hand. He feels inadequate, and it makes him angry, so he tries to make Jesus angry. He hasn't learned yet that it doesn't work."

Mary leaned back against his chest, taking comfort from his nearness and his strength. "Why can't he just be thankful that he has such a wonderful brother?"

"He may, in time."

The next day they set off with a multitude of the townspeople going toward Jerusalem. It was a time of celebration and rejoicing as they remembered their deliverance from Egypt. There was much laughter and song as they traveled. The group separated into smaller groups, changing as time went on. At first Jesus stayed close to Mary and Joseph; then He was drawn away to a group of boys His own age.

Mary slowed her walk a bit to keep pace with an older woman who still made the trip each year. Mary tried to give what help she could, offering to carry the woman's load. Rachel smiled at her but refused to give up her burden.

"Maybe in a day or two I will be willing to let you carry it for me, but for now when I am fresh, I want to carry it myself." Then she chuckled. "Every day it gets lighter, though, as I eat some of what I am carrying!"

Mary laughed with her, and they talked of life in the village and of mutual acquaintances.

The weather was perfect for travel. It was not yet hot enough to make them uncomfortable, yet it was warm enough that they didn't suffer from the cold as they camped for the night. Jesus joined Mary and Joseph at their own campfire each night. Other boys were on their own, but Mary insisted that she would rest more comfortably if He was with them. He didn't complain about it, even when the other boys made a point of coming to ask if He could stay with their group. Joseph kindly explained to them that they had decided to camp together. He added, after a brief consultation with Mary, "But you are welcome to join us at our fire, if you wish."

The days of travel passed quickly with so much to keep them occupied. Soon they could see Jerusalem in the distance. The boys who were going for the first time grew silent and rejoined their own family groups. The awesomeness of what they were celebrating was becoming clear to them.

Mary remembered her first time at the Passover celebration. She had been overwhelmed by the knowledge that God cared about them; that He had chosen them for His own people; that He had delivered them from the oppression of Pharaoh by His direct intervention; that He led them by His presence through the wilderness; and that He had made provision for them to become a great nation. Now He was preparing a deliverer for them again. They would have their own king once more, as in the days of long ago.

Her left hand was nestled in Joseph's, and her right hand found Jesus' hand. They joined the others in the songs of the ascents as they neared the temple. She could feel Jesus' hand trembling as they approached the temple. She looked at Him with concern, but it was expectancy and awe on His face rather than the fear and nervousness she thought she would see.

The sudden realization came to her that this son of hers was coming into His Father's house for the first time that He would remember. A stab of pain shot through her. *Will He still consider Himself to be my firstborn son? Will He begin to pull away from me?*

As though He was aware of her turmoil He turned to smile at her and squeezed her hand slightly.

She returned the smile, and the familiar peacefulness flooded through her. The Passover celebrations were more meaningful to her this year, knowing that God was still at work and that He was preparing another deliverance for them.

They met with friends in Jerusalem to celebrate the first day of the feast before going to the temple. They sacrificed a lamb, roasted it with herbs, and ate together.

The feast began with the familiar words "This is the bread of affliction that our fathers ate in the land of Egypt. Whoever is hungry, let him come and eat; whoever is in need, let him come and conduct the Seder of Passover. This year we are here; next year in the land of Israel. This year we are slaves; next year we will be free people."

As was the custom, the youngest child asked his father, "Why is this night different from all other nights?

"On all other nights, we eat either unleavened or leavened bread, but tonight we eat only unleavened bread.

"On all other nights, we eat all kinds of vegetables, but tonight we eat only bitter herbs.

"On all other nights, we do not dip our food even once, but tonight we dip twice.

"On all other nights, we eat either sitting or reclining, but tonight we all recline."

The answer came back, "We do this because of what the Lord did for us when we left Egypt."

They spent the week visiting with friends, sharing meals, and, when they were safely out of earshot of the officials, talking of the oppression by Rome and the coming deliverance by the Messiah.

On the last day of the feast Joseph took Mary and Jesus to the temple, where they presented their sacrifice to God. Jesus asked for permission to speak to the officials in the temple, and permission was given.

Some of his friends came to Mary and Joseph, asking if Jesus would be allowed to accompany them for the beginning of their trip back to Nazareth. Permission was also given for this, as long as He came back to their fire at night.

After the celebrations they set out for home. As they prepared to set up their camp for the night, Jesus did not show up. Mary stayed at the campfire, and Joseph made the rounds to the families of His friends. When Joseph came back alone, Mary was afraid. Jesus' friends hadn't seen Him since they started their homeward journey.

"Where can He be? How could we travel so far and not miss Him? What kind of a mother am I to lose my son? To lose God's Son? O God, I am so sorry. You must know where He is. Please keep Him safe until we can get to Him."

Without even taking the time to eat, they set off for Jerusalem again. At dawn they made their way to the temple, and there they found Jesus, surrounded by the temple leaders and teachers. They were deep in conversation.

Mary rushed up to Him. "We thought You were with us on the road home. We have been so worried about You! Why didn't You let us know You were going to stay behind to talk to these men?"

Jesus turned to her. "I'm sorry you were concerned. I thought you would know where I would be. I have to begin doing My Father's work."

Mary held back her tears until they were outside. Then she let them flow. Joseph led her to a seat outside the temple where she could get herself back in hand. Jesus sat beside her, His arm around her shoulder.

"I thought I had lost You. I was given You to care for, and I lost You. What must God think of me? What kind of a mother would forget her own son?"

Jesus replied, "God knew you were the only one who could be My mother. He chose well. He knew before He chose you that this would happen, and yet He allowed it. No harm has come to Me. Perhaps He wants you to know that He is looking after Me as well, that your responsibility is growing less as I get older. I have decisions to make about His work and about the future. I must learn all I can." Jesus spoke quietly, calmly, and kindly, and Mary soon stopped crying.

After a short rest and a meal, they resumed their journey. Since there were only the three of them, they were able to travel at a quicker pace than when they were with the whole group, but still, by the time they caught up to the rest of the travelers they were less than a day's journey from Nazareth.

During the last day on the road, Mary spent much time in thought. She was coming to terms with her son growing up. *What He said makes a lot of sense. He is my son, but He's also*

God's Son, a special person, chosen to be the king, the Messiah, the deliverer. He will have to prepare for that. Her mind raced as she thought about all the possibilities. *He'll have to be trained for leadership, won't He? How will He raise an army without making the Romans angry? Will many people die in the rebellion that will surely come? At least, since He will be the king, He won't be killed.*

Without warning, like a bolt of lightning through her thoughts, God spoke to her through the Scriptures. "'For my thoughts are not your thoughts, neither are your ways my ways,' declares the LORD. 'As the heavens are higher than the earth, so are my ways higher than your ways and my thoughts than your thoughts.'"

For a while she pondered the meaning of the words. Jesus was the Messiah, the deliverer, the king. She remembered what Simeon had said on their first visit to the temple when Jesus was a baby: "A sword will pierce your own soul too." He had spoken as though a sword would pierce Jesus. Why would that happen to the king? How could that happen to God's Son?

She was so deep in thought that she wasn't paying attention to the road, and she stumbled over a stone. Jesus took her by the arm and asked if she was all right. She looked deep into His eyes, trying to read His thoughts.

"I will be fine. I didn't fall; I just stumbled."

"You have been thinking very deeply," He said.

"Yes, I have been going over what You said to me outside the temple and thinking about things that happened when You were a baby and about what is to come, trying to sort everything out."

"Is that what you're supposed to be doing? Sorting things out? Isn't that the work of God?"

He spoke with respect, but she heard the rebuke from God. She smiled at Him. "No, that's not what I'm supposed to be doing. I'm supposed to be rejoicing in the presence of my son while He's with me. I'm supposed to be enjoying the company along the road and remembering the celebration we just left in Jerusalem. If I was supposed to be sorting things out, I wouldn't have stumbled."

They laughed as they continued on their way, but deep in her heart, she knew their relationship had changed. He was no longer her little boy. He was on the way to becoming the man God had sent Him to be.

nine

FOR A FEW MONTHS AFTER THEY RETURNED, THINGS CONTINUED as before. Jesus helped Joseph in the carpenter shop. Mary could hear them having long discussions as she and her mother trained the girls in their tasks and chores.

She was not surprised when at breakfast one morning Jesus asked permission from Joseph to go into the hills alone for the day.

"I have to be alone to think about the things I learned in Jerusalem and the things we have been speaking of and the Scriptures I've learned at the synagogue."

Joseph was silent for a time before he answered, "Yes, if You feel the need, then it is time for You to go."

Mary prepared a small lunch for Him to take, and He carried water with Him as well. As the day passed, her eyes often strayed to the path He had taken into the hills. When she saw Him returning at the end of the day, she forced herself to remain at the house, knowing that if He was able to share His thoughts, He would. When the younger children were sleeping, He talked to Joseph, Mary, Anna and Joses.

"I will stay in the carpenter shop until it is time for Me to go. I don't know for sure yet when that will be, but by then Joses will be working with you full-time as well."

Joses was certainly gifted with his hands, and he had already proved a capable helper. He still attended the synagogue school during the day, but he helped in the shop at every opportunity.

The years continued on. Often Jesus would take a day or two to go into the hills alone. Sometimes He took some of His brothers with Him. Joses chose not to go, but James and Judah would go whenever they had the chance.

Anna had been growing steadily more feeble but tried to keep doing what she could to help. One morning, she did not awaken with the rest of the family. She had died in her sleep. They were sad to lose her, but they knew it was a part of life to die.

Mary and the girls prepared her for burial. Since she had died in their home, they were all considered unclean, so they stayed to themselves for the necessary week until the ritual cleansing was completed.

A few weeks after Anna's death, Joses cried out to his mother from the shop. She ran in and saw Joseph crumpled in a heap on the floor.

"He just grabbed his chest and fell," explained Joses, trying to raise his father from the floor. Jesus came in from the back of the house to help. But Mary knew that her husband was dead. A cold numbness settled over her. She efficiently told the young men where to place the body of their father. Again they prepared a body for burial, and again they went through the period of uncleanness and the cleansing.

Gradually the numbness began to wear off as Mary realized that never again would she be able to gather strength from this man who had been by her side through so many years. His calming influence had helped her through rough times too numerous to mention. The presence of her children, although a help, could not make up for the emptiness she saw stretching before her. For a time she withdrew into herself, going through the motions of living but not really experiencing life. It was her firstborn son, her deliverer, who truly brought deliverance to her.

"Mother, today I want you to come with Me into the hills. I want you to see where I go when I need to be alone with My Father. It can be a secret place for you as well, if you wish."

They walked without speaking along the path behind the house. The terrain was rocky, but the path was clear. As the village disappeared behind them, so did all sounds of human life. They could hear the wind, the birds, and the insects, but all else was silent. The sun was hot. The breeze kept the flies from becoming too thick around them.

Jesus led her to a place where there was a small tree, so there was shelter from the blazing sun. She sat on a rock looking out over the valley to the northeast. She could see sparkles where the sun was reflecting on the Sea of Galilee in the distance.

The words of a psalm ran through her head. She spoke them, and Jesus joined her.

"I love the LORD, for he heard my voice; he heard my cry for mercy. Because he turned his ear to me, I will call on him as long as I live. The cords of death entangled me, the anguish of the grave came upon me; I was overcome by trouble and sorrow. Then I called on the name of the LORD: 'O LORD, save me!'"

They continued through the psalm, exclaiming triumphantly at the end, "Praise the LORD!"

For several hours they sat, talking about Joseph's life, listening quietly to the sounds around them, sharing memories of their life as a family, laughing about the antics of the younger children as they were growing up. By the time they decided to head back home, Mary was beginning to heal. She felt renewed and refreshed.

She placed her hand on Jesus' arm. "Thank You for sharing Your day and Your secret place with me. It will become a refuge for me in times to come. God is here, isn't He?"

"Yes, He is. But then, wherever His people are, He is there as well. Sometimes we have to get away from the noise and the distraction of every day to really hear Him speak to us."

As the firstborn son, Jesus was assumed to be the heir of both the home and the business. He did spend much time in the carpenter shop, but He and Joses both knew that Joses would be the one to continue the business. They worked together for months at a time. Then Jesus would be called away again to spend time alone in the hills. Sometimes Mary would go part of the way with Him, to spend time alone on her own hilltop. She unfailingly heard God speaking to her through the stillness and majesty of His creation.

By now, all of the other children of Mary and Joseph had married. Joses' wife had moved into the family home with them, and the other sons lived nearby. Their girls, Hannah, Elisabeth, and Rebekah, were a bit farther away but within a few days' walk. Mary spent time in each of their homes. Jesus was still a part of Joses' household, but His absences were becoming longer and more frequent.

ten

"HAVE YOU HEARD ABOUT THE NEW PROPHET? HIS NAME IS John, and he's saying that he's the herald of the Messiah." The news was being told over and over with different variations.

Mary had been waiting to hear about John. She had been present at his birth thirty years earlier. She knew he would be proclaiming the coming of the king. Things were about to start happening.

Jesus had left a few weeks earlier to go into the hills and spend time alone with His Father. He had told her that He would probably be heading for the area around the Jordan River when He came back from the wilderness.

Late in the day a young man named Josiah appeared at the house, asking for Mary. "Your daughter Hannah would like to see you. She's due to give birth soon and would like you to be with her."

Mary gathered a few of her belongings and left the next morning with Josiah, who was the brother of Hannah's husband, Reuben. She gladly left the household in the capable hands of Judith, Joses' wife. As she left, she turned to Judith and said, "If Jesus comes back here before He goes on, tell Him I'm visiting Hannah on the other side of Jericho."

For three days they traveled. Mary was impatient to arrive

at Hannah's home before the anticipated baby arrived, but Josiah insisted that they take the journey slowly and carefully so they would have no accidents. Mary recognized his wisdom, but inwardly she chafed at what seemed to her an unnecessarily slow pace. As the time went on, she began to understand his thinking. Apart from the fact that she was older than he was, the road became rougher, and the terrain was hilly. Finally she admitted to him that his idea had been a good one.

He laughed. "Did you think I couldn't see your impatience? I have been traveling this road for years, and I know how difficult it can be if you start off too fast. I also know human nature, and if I tell people that the way grows harder, they think they will be used to it by the time they get to the rough part, not realizing that the quicker pace wears them out. You have been a good traveler, though. Even though you were impatient, you still had the wisdom to let me lead."

Now it was Mary's turn to laugh. "And I thought I was being so careful about hiding my impatience!"

By the middle of the third day, they were coming close to Jericho. In the distance, Mary could see two people approaching. As they drew nearer, she recognized Hannah and Reuben. Mary ran to meet her daughter and hugged her, laughing as the baby kicked in protest.

"How did you know we would be so close?" she asked.

Reuben answered, "We know how long it takes Josiah to make the journey, and we knew he would be more determined than you were to keep his pace, so I told Hannah we could start out today to meet you along the way."

Mary gave him a hug. "Thank you for being so understanding."

Reuben laughed. "I really didn't have much of a choice. I didn't want Hannah to come by herself, and she just wasn't willing to wait any longer." His arm encircled his wife, and she rested her head against his shoulder.

The rest of the journey was an easy one, as Mary and Hannah were both content in each other's company. After they arrived, Hannah proudly showed her mother the garments she had painstakingly made for her baby.

Later in the day, Mary asked how Hannah had had enough energy to meet her.

Hannah replied, "This morning when I woke up, I was so full of energy, I felt like I could have walked all the way to Nazareth!"

Mary laughed. "I remember saying something very much like that the morning before Jesus was born. This little one will be here very soon, I think."

During the evening meal, Hannah's eyes widened, and she stopped talking in the middle of a sentence. Then she gasped, "I think the baby is ready to be born!"

Before the sun rose the next morning, the cry of a newborn filled the house. Mary wrapped the tiny girl and passed her to her father to hold while she saw to Hannah's needs. When Hannah was presentable, Reuben carefully passed the baby to her mother.

He sat down weakly, shaking his head. "That was the hardest work I've done in a long time."

Mary and Hannah laughed. Mary assured him that he would soon become accustomed to handling the newborn, and although his eyes expressed disbelief, he didn't put it into words.

Mary gave Hannah time to examine the baby carefully, to cuddle her close and whisper to her as she nursed, before she took her to clean her.

For several days Mary helped Hannah, enjoying the time she got to spend with her newest grandchild. Finally they became aware of what was going on around them. The rumors were flying about the prophet at the Jordan River who was calling for people to repent and be baptized. Some thought he was Elijah, come back from the dead; others thought he was the Messiah. Hannah asked Mary if she thought John was the Messiah. Mary told her honestly and frankly that Jesus, her brother, was God's chosen Messiah.

Hannah laughed. "Mother, I'm serious."

Mary replied, "So am I." Then she went through the whole story again of how the angel had appeared to her, how the same angel had gone to Joseph in a dream and told him the same things. How she had visited with Elisabeth and had been present at the birth of John; of the miraculous way Elisabeth had conceived after being childless for so many years; how Zacharias had not been allowed to speak through the whole pregnancy because of his unbelief; how his voice had been restored after the birth of John; of the angels appearing to the shepherds the night Jesus was born; of the angel appearing to Joseph and telling them to leave Bethlehem just before Herod killed the babies.

Hannah spoke softly. "You told us this when we were growing up, but it seemed like a made-up story, something to put us to sleep at night. I never really believed it until now. I always thought my father was Jesus' father."

"We weren't sure how much to tell and how much to keep secret. We didn't want the wrong people to find out, in case they came after Jesus, but then we knew that God would protect Him. We weren't careless, but we did want His family to know who He was…is."

"Jesus always was our champion when we were small. He was so kind and loving and always so obedient. It annoyed Joses sometimes, but I was thankful that I had a brother who cared about me more than He cared about what others thought of Him. He is God's Son. That is so incredible! It is going to take some time before I can get that into my mind."

Mary replied with a smile, "I've known for thirty years, and it's still hard to realize."

The next morning a group of neighbors decided it was time for them to go check out this prophet at the Jordan River. Hannah was unable to go but asked Mary to please go, remember everything, and come back and tell her all about it. Mary set out with a growing excitement, knowing that the things they had been looking forward to were now happening.

As they approached the river, they could hear John's voice booming through the air. "Don't try to get by as you are, thinking, 'We're safe because we are descendants of Abraham.' That proves nothing. God could turn these stones into descendants of Abraham!"

For a while his voice was quieter, as though he had turned away from them. Then they heard him again. "Someone else is coming, someone so great that I am not even worthy to carry His shoes. He will baptize you with the Holy Spirit and with fire."

Again there was silence. Then they could hear two voices in conversation. Someone was asking John to baptize him. John protested, "But *I* need to be baptized by *You*. It doesn't seem right for *me* to baptize *You*."

Her first sight of John was a shock. He was dressed in rough skins, and his hair was unkempt. She thought, *No wonder they think he is Elijah!* By this time Mary could see that John was speaking to Jesus. She stayed where she could see and hear without being seen.

Jesus spoke again. "I must do what is right. Please baptize Me."

John took Him down into the river and baptized Him. As soon as Jesus came up out of the water, a shape like a dove came down to Him, and a voice could be heard saying, "This is My dearly loved Son. I am very pleased with Him."

Mary dropped to her knees in awe. She had heard the voice of God claiming His Son—and her son. When she looked up, the people were staring around uncertainly. John's face shone, and there were a few others who also seemed overcome, but there were others who murmured about the noise. They had heard no voice. When asked about the dove, they said they just saw a movement of light and shadow.

As Jesus made His way through the crowd to leave, He saw Mary and came toward her. Her face was still shining, and she smiled through her tears as she hugged Him.

"My dearly loved son," she repeated.

He returned the hug and whispered, "I must go now. My ministry is beginning."

"When will I see You again?"

"I'm not sure. I will be around Galilee soon."

"God go with You."

"And with You." Then He was gone.

Mary moved forward to listen to what John had to say. "That was the one I have been telling you about. He is the Lamb of God who will take away the sin of the world."

The people listened quietly as John continued to talk to them about changing their ways, about becoming what God was asking them to be, of *being* holy and not just *acting* holy.

When John had finished speaking many of the people began to leave. Mary sat quietly, thinking about the events of the day and the precious few moments with her son. The words "My dearly loved Son," kept going through her mind. She loved Him so much, she would gladly give her life for

Him, even now. She bowed her head and silently prayed for Him.

"Oh Lord God, protect my son—Your Son—as He does Your work. Lead Him; show Him Your will. Give Him the strength to do Your will no matter what. Give me the wisdom to do what You want me to do. Help me to always be a help, not a hindrance. Don't let me stand in His way. Give me the strength and courage to face whatever comes."

As she glanced up, John was standing before her. He knelt down and looked into her face.

"God has given me the gift of knowing who needs to repent. You gave yourself to Him a long time ago. Have you ever questioned His ways?"

Mary answered with a laugh. "At least a million times. But I realize He knows better than I do about everything, so I'm obedient, even when I don't understand."

John smiled. From what Mary had heard about him, it was a rare thing. Then he spoke again.

"Have we met before? You seem to be someone I know."

Mary smiled. "Yes, we have met…at your birth. I stayed with your mother in the months before you were born. I was the first person to hold you. The last time I saw you was when you were about two weeks old."

"You? Then that was—" John turned his head in the direction Jesus had gone.

"Yes, He is my son."

He pulled her to her feet and enveloped her in a hug before he strode away to the hills.

Mary rejoined the few remaining stragglers from Jericho as they headed back home, staying a bit apart from them, trying to sort out her thoughts. What would be important to tell Hannah about the day? She tried to recall the things John had said to everyone, but what he had said to her made more of an impression on her thoughts. What Jesus had said and done was the most important. Could she communicate how she felt without making Hannah feel she wasn't loved as much as Jesus was? *Were* her other children loved as much as He was? They certainly were loved greatly. It was just that Jesus was special. It was almost as though the roles were reversed where He was concerned. She felt a great love and caring from Him as though from her father. She knew there was no way she could explain it adequately, and she knew that was the main problem with Joses. He had never understood the difference between himself and Jesus.

The love she felt for the children of Joseph was in no way diminished by the love she felt for the child of God.

One of the younger men of the group dropped back to talk to Mary as they walked.

"I noticed that the man who was baptized came to talk to you. He even gave you a hug. You must know Him."

"Yes. He is my son."

"And then the prophet was talking to you as well."

Mary smiled. She hadn't realized how closely she had been observed. "He's a relative of my family. I stayed with his mother when he was born."

The young man persisted. "Did you hear a voice?"

Mary replied with a question of her own. "Did you?"

The man looked almost ashamed. "Yes, the voice clearly said, 'This is My dearly loved Son.'"

Mary placed her hand on his arm in encouragement. "I heard the voice as well."

"But you said He was *your* son. Wasn't that God's voice speaking? How could you have God's child?"

For the second time in two days Mary found herself retelling the story of the appearance of the angel, Joseph's dream, the visit to Elisabeth, the trip to Bethlehem, the visits from the shepherds and the wise men, and the escape to Egypt, all at God's direction.

"Then the prophecies that Isaiah wrote about a virgin having a child were literally true. He wasn't speaking figuratively. That means our deliverance is coming!" The young man was becoming more and more excited as he talked, as though everything that he had learned was beginning to fall into place.

eleven

MARY WAS ABLE TO SORT OUT THE IMPORTANT THINGS THAT HAD happened to tell Hannah. After staying with her for a few more weeks, she headed home to Nazareth. There was going to be a wedding in the family, and she wanted to be on hand to help.

The week of the wedding celebrations arrived. Mary had been almost living at the home of her cousin in the final days. Her cousin and his family were well-known and liked in the surrounding area. The bride's family had a large connection as well. The guest list was long, but she thought the preparations had been adequate.

As the party continued, Mary became concerned that the food supply was not going to last. She hurriedly gave instructions to her daughters and daughters-in-law to prepare more. Then the man in charge of the wine came to her.

"We are on the last container of wine, and the guests show no sign of stopping. What should we do?"

For a brief moment of panic she wanted to scream, "Why are you asking me?"

She took a deep breath, closed her eyes and prayed silently, "O God, I know this doesn't seem like a major crisis to You, but it is so important to these people. This is their wedding, and they want things to go right. Show me what to do."

With no clear idea of how things would work out, she spoke to the man. "Leave it with me. Don't worry."

As she turned her head, she saw Jesus arrive with a few of His friends. Immediately she began to relax. She pulled Him aside.

"Jesus, they are running out of wine. You know how important this occasion is to Jacob and his family. Can you do something?"

"What am I supposed to do?"

She smiled and turned to the servants. "Whatever He tells you to do, don't question; just do it."

She heard Him ask the servants to fill the waterpots that were sitting nearby. When that was done, He asked them to take some to the man in charge. A few minutes later, the man came rushing to Mary.

"Usually, people serve the best wine first and save the poorer quality until later, but this is the best wine I have ever tasted! Where did you have it stored? I couldn't find any anywhere."

"Call it a gift from God," she replied.

She became aware of the whisperings of the guests. The servants and the friends of Jesus were aware of how the wine had come to be. They were so excited by the miracle, they couldn't keep it to themselves. In the midst of her rejoicing there came a stab of pain. Things had changed now to the point where Jesus would never again be just her son. His anonymity was gone; His privacy was gone. For a few seconds she became angry, wanting to hide Him away from the people who would have Him made a display for their own selfish ends.

As she had become so accustomed to doing, she turned to God with her jumbled emotions. "God, please calm me down. I know there is nothing more I can do to protect Him from the world. Help me to support Him in prayer. Give me wisdom to say and do the right things. If You want me to keep quiet, tell me. If You want me to speak, tell me. If You want me to act, tell me. If You want me to do nothing, tell me. I am so afraid of getting in the way and making a mistake."

Unmistakably the answer came. "I will give you peace and wisdom. Trust Me with My Son."

"Yes, God, I do trust You. Thank You for Your help again." Mary smiled and went back to the celebrations.

After the guests had departed and things were put to rights, Jesus approached His mother.

"We're going to Capernaum for a few days. Do you want to come with us? You've been working very hard, and I think you need a bit of a change."

Mary was delighted to agree. She knew her time with her firstborn would be limited from now on, and she would treasure every moment she could spend with Him. She was happy for another reason as well. Although Jesus was the oldest son and heir, He was absent from their home much of the time, and Joses and his wife looked at the house and shop as theirs. Joses still felt animosity toward Jesus, and since Mary seemed to be so wrapped up in everything He did, the hard feelings spilled over to her. She found herself trying to spend more and more time away from her home and with her other children.

She spent a memorable time with Jesus, James, and some of their friends, walking and talking, sitting and listening to Jesus talk to them. She was amazed all over again at His wisdom and His understanding of how things were and how they should be. He used everyday objects and scenes to teach them lessons about God and their relationship with Him. In one unforgettable lesson He taught them that He was the root and stem of a tree and they were the branches. Their responsibility was to allow His life to flow through them to provide nourishment and produce lives that would show His life in them. Mary pondered that lesson for hours, studying how the branches just hung there, not working on their own, not striving to produce fruit, not making decisions on how to best accomplish their purpose. They simply acted as a channel for the life-producing, life-sustaining sap that flowed from the root and finally produced fruit.

She slipped away from the group to allow the lesson to sink in, to become a part of her. All alone, she raised her arms to the sky and prayed, "O God, I thank You for showing me the freedom in giving myself to You completely. All these years, I thought I had, but I was still trying to work on my own, still doing and not just being. Keep reminding me. Don't let me ever forget this lesson."

By the time she returned to the group, they were resting or talking quietly among themselves. Jesus sat slightly apart from them, so she made her way to Him. He shifted slightly to allow her to sit beside Him on the rock. His arm went around her shoulders, and she rested her head briefly on His shoulder.

She spoke quietly. "You have taught me so much in the past few days, I don't think I will ever be the same. You have shown me that there should be nothing of my own working or striving, but that I should be simply a vessel through which God can accomplish His purpose, for His glory. I feel so light and so free."

His arm tightened around her. Then He threw back His head and laughed, a hearty, joyful laugh that echoed through the hills where they were sitting. He stood up and pulled Mary to her feet. His arms went around her, and He swung her in a circle, the both of them overcome with laughter. When He sat her back on her feet, He placed His right hand on her cheek and spoke so that only she could hear.

"My dear little mother, you have always been such a source of strength and comfort to Me. Even now, when I have begun My ministry, My Father is still using you to encourage Me. I was wondering if anything I had said over the past few days was getting through to anyone. You have calmed My doubts by sharing with Me the lesson I was trying to teach."

Tears formed in Mary's eyes and ran down her cheeks as she smiled at her son.

They made their way back to Nazareth, and Jesus stayed in their home for a few days. Joses' attitude was worse than usual. He condemned Jesus for neglecting the family business and criticized Mary for encouraging Him.

One day, when Jesus had gone to the hills behind the house, Joses approached Mary in anger. "He's the oldest son. *He's* supposed to be the head of the family. Instead He goes off on these trips to who knows where. He's lazy! He has no sense of responsibility."

When Mary tried to explain that Jesus was not Joseph's son but God's and had a ministry from His Father to fulfill, Joses lost his temper, shouting that she was deluded, that Jesus was insane.

"How dare you pass off your sin and your illegitimate son as God's child! I don't know how you ever convinced my father to believe such a lie, but I don't accept it."

Before Mary could even react, a sense of peace came over her. She stood silently, looking at him for a few seconds, before turning away. She sought out her familiar solitary place away from the house. As she sat, going over the conversation in her mind, anger surged to the forefront, and she longed to lash out at Joses, to punish him for his disrespect of God, of his brother and of her.

The still voice of God came through her anger and hurt. "He doesn't understand yet. Leave him to Me."

A sound behind her startled her, and she whipped around to see Jesus striding along the path.

He spoke before she had a chance to say anything. "It has happened already, hasn't it? I knew it would come, but I thought I would have more time. There is no sense in trying to convince him. It will just make him more angry right now. Can you stay with Rebekah and Nathan?"

They made their way slowly back toward the house. Joses was just leaving the shop with his latest order, but he didn't see them. His wife was not at home, so Mary and Jesus were able to gather their belongings without interference.

Mary said, "We can let him know we won't be bothering him anymore when we get settled at Rebekah's, if Nathan will let us stay." She looked around at the familiar surroundings. This had been her home for all of her married life, except when they were in Bethlehem and Egypt. It was hard now to leave, but she knew it would have been even harder, if not impossible, to stay.

twelve

FOR A FEW DAYS MARY STAYED WITH HER DAUGHTER REBEKAH. The house was small, and with Rebekah and Nathan's two children, it was crowded. Nathan was a kind, loving husband and father, with a strong faith in God. He was searching for the truth, and he accepted that the prophecies had been fulfilled and the Messiah had come.

Jesus spent time with them but did not sleep at the house, preferring to spend the time alone with His Father. When He was at the house, He and Nathan talked of things present and the things to come.

On the Sabbath, Jesus and Nathan went to the synagogue together. The two little ones were sick, so Mary and Rebekah stayed at home with them. Several hours later, Nathan came rushing in alone.

"Has Jesus come back here?" he asked. His eyes were wide and dark, and he was out of breath.

Immediately Rebekah became alarmed. "What's happened? Where have you been? What's going on?"

Mary sat quietly, holding the baby. Her head was bowed so it rested against the top of Naomi's soft little head. She prayed silently for peace and safety for the little family and for strength to bear what was to come.

Nathan recounted the events that had unfolded at the synagogue. Jesus had read from the prophet Isaiah and then talked to them about it. They were skeptical because He had grown up among them. They all knew Him. He couldn't be anyone special. The more He talked, the more sense He made, and the angrier they became. A mob had formed and tried to drag Him to the cliff to throw Him off, but somehow He had managed to get away.

"Was Joses there?" Mary had to know.

Nathan hesitated, but Mary could read on his face what he didn't want to tell her. She knew he had been one of the leaders of the mob. To ease his embarrassment, she added, "Never mind. I already know."

"I don't know where Jesus has gone, but I thought I had better come here, in case He had come back, and in case they decide to look for Him here. I was going to warn Him to hide."

Mary's eyes were soft as she spoke. "He wouldn't put you in danger. He won't come back here. Perhaps I should go as well before they come. When they do come, let them look through, to prove to themselves that He isn't here. Don't try to fight them."

After quick, fierce hugs, Mary took her belongings and fled to the hills behind Nazareth. She needed time to gather her thoughts, to pray and seek God's leading. She found her spot, her favorite rock, and sat quietly, listening to the birds and to the wind in the shrubbery. A portion of the writings of Isaiah came to her mind. *"This is what the Sovereign LORD, the Holy One of Israel, says: 'In repentance and rest is your salvation, in quietness and trust is your strength...' The LORD longs to be gracious to you; he rises to show you compassion. For the LORD is a God of justice. Blessed are all who wait for him!"*

She had her answer. She would wait for Jesus to come to her there, if it took the rest of the day. She prayed for Joses and for Jesus and the rest of her family, but especially for Joses. She wanted him to find the peace that she had in knowing that Jesus was their long-awaited Messiah. She wanted him to recognize the treasure he had in living with God's Son for all of his life. She wanted—and she wondered if it was selfish on her part—peace and harmony in her family.

The sun was beginning to sink toward the horizon before she heard footsteps on the path behind her. She turned, expecting to see Jesus approaching, but it was James. She could see the concern in his eyes as he approached.

"Here you are!" he exclaimed in relief. He gave her a quick hug. "We've been so concerned about you after what happened today. Rebekah sent me to look for you. Jesus got word to them that He was going down to the Sea of Galilee. They knew you wouldn't have heard."

"Did anybody go to Nathan's house?"

"Yes, but they were calmer by the time they arrived. They didn't even wake the little ones." He tried to hide a smile. "I think Rebekah could have handled the whole mob by herself. She was determined they wouldn't disturb the two little ones, and they listened to her!"

"Did they check the house?"

"Yes, Nathan insisted that one or two of their choosing look through quietly. After that, they just left. It was about an hour later when they got word from Jesus. Then Rebekah sent Nathan to tell me to find you. They think it would be safe for you to come back—just for tonight, if you don't want to stay longer."

"It isn't a matter of wanting to stay; it's a matter of safety for them. I don't want to bring trouble on them. I'll go back to visit with Hannah again for a while."

They walked quickly back to Nathan's house. By the time they arrived, it was fully dark. They stopped a short distance from the house to talk.

"Mother, don't leave until I come. I will travel with you to Hannah's. Then I am going to find Jesus."

"But He is beginning His ministry."

"Yes, I know, and He is going to need some help. I have to do this. I can't explain it, but I know it is right for me to go."

Mary hugged him. "My dear son, if God is leading you in that direction, then that's the way you have to go. There is no way around it. Just be sure."

James replied, "I am sure. I have heard Jesus teach. I have listened to John at the Jordan River. I know."

Mary held him close for a long time, allowing her emotions to settle. Finally she was able to say, "You remind me so much of your father. When he knew something was right, there was no stopping him."

In the darkness and the silence, she told Rebekah and Nathan that she would be leaving the next morning.

"Mother," Rebekah began, "it isn't necessary. You can stay here. Tell her, Nathan."

Mary interrupted. "As long as I stay here, the authorities will be watching not just me but you as well. You don't need the added danger when you have your two little ones to think about. I will be safe with Hannah, away from this village where they remember Jesus as a child."

Shortly after daylight the next day, James returned for her, and the two of them left the village. Their journey took them three days. Mary remembered the journey she had made such a short time before to visit Hannah. So much had happened so quickly, it seemed as though a lifetime had passed.

Hannah and Reuben were surprised but delighted to see them. They talked for hours, the fading daylight unnoticed. Reuben insisted that Mary and James could stay with them for as long as they wanted.

As soon as it was light, James left to find Jesus. Mary and Hannah visited, catching up on family news and the growth of Reuben and Hannah's Sarah. Hannah said that Reuben had been to see John at the Jordan and had been very different ever since. He had been kinder and more considerate, and he had begun studying the scrolls at the synagogue, talking to the rabbi and some of the other teachers.

As the days and weeks passed, rumors began spreading about the new teacher who could perform miracles. After hearing a particularly spectacular story about a dead girl being brought back to life, Mary sighed.

"They are just following Him for the show!" she exclaimed in exasperation. "They don't want truth; they just want to be entertained."

Daily they would hear stories of things that had happened, people healed, His chosen followers sent out to talk to the people. They wondered aloud when He was going to take up arms against the government.

In the midst of the speculation came the shocking news of John's death. Mary was stunned when she heard. "How could someone chosen by God to spread His message be killed? Wasn't God protecting him? Does this mean Jesus is also in danger? John wasn't plotting against the government. Why was he killed? Has Jesus heard about it? How does He feel? Where is He?"

As always, she took her doubts and fears to God. He gave her peace in the midst of her uncertainty. Then she went to Reuben. "Have you heard where Jesus is?"

"Yes, He's gone north again, up around Galilee."

"Does He know about John?"

"Someone said His disciples came for John's body, so He must know. They would have told Him."

The next news they heard was that Jesus had fed thousands of people. Multitudes of people began following Him after that. They were saying they would no longer have to work. Everything would be provided. They would beat the Romans right back to where they came from. They had a leader who could do anything, even provide their daily food.

Mary continued to live with Hannah and Reuben, helping with Sarah and then with baby Reuben.

One morning when Hannah was preparing the midday meal and Mary was busy with Sarah, they heard a man calling to them.

Hannah ran to the door to welcome the dear friends that had come to visit.

"Mother, this is Lazarus, and his sisters, Martha and Mary."

Mary found herself enveloped in warm hugs as the introductions were made.

"We've come to share a meal with you," Martha began, "but we have not come empty-handed. May I help you get this food set out for everyone?"

Hannah laughed as she welcomed Martha's help and food. "I might have known you would bring enough for everyone!"

Mary was able to study the three guests as they shared the meal. She guessed that Martha was the oldest of the three and Mary was the youngest. None of the three had any gray hair, so she knew they were younger than she was. There was such a strong family resemblance, it was almost amusing, with the women being feminine counterparts of their brother. They all had wide-set brown eyes, strong chins, straight dark hair and rather large noses. The women's eyebrows were not quite as full and bushy as their brother's, but they were certainly fuller than most women's.

Martha carried the conversation as well as doing most of the work. *A force to be reckoned with,* thought Mary with a smile. As she smiled, her eyes caught those of the other Mary, and they shared a glimmer of instant recognition of a kindred spirit.

When the meal ended, Martha shooed everyone except Hannah away while they cleaned up the remains of the meal. Lazarus and Reuben disappeared along the trail behind the house, and the Marys took the little ones out to sit in the shade of the house. As always, Sarah stayed close to her grandmother, while the other Mary took charge of the almost sleeping baby, Reuben.

"How far away do you live?" Mary the elder asked.

"Just an easy walk. Not too far," Mary the younger replied. "In fact, we make the trip at least once a week when the weather is favorable. It's so good to find friends who share our beliefs and who are looking forward to the redemption of Israel."

Mary was startled. "What do you mean?"

"The belief in our promised Messiah. We believe He is already here," Mary the younger explained.

"Do you know who He is?" Mary the elder asked quietly.

Mary the younger's voice dropped to a whisper. "Yes. He is Jesus."

Mary the elder reached out and grasped her hand. "I know Him too. He is my son."

Mary the younger reached out to give her a hug, waking the now sleeping baby. As she gently rocked him in her arms to put him back to sleep, Mary the elder began to speak.

She had lost count of the number of times she had shared the story of the visit of the angel and all the other signs and assurances they had been given, but she told it again with joy and gladness, knowing that here was someone who believed because of the work of God, not just because she had seen the signs and miracles.

As time and opportunity permitted, she made trips to visit with Jesus when He was within a day's journey. Often she met Him in Bethany at the home of Lazarus, Mary and Martha. They brought word when Jesus was going to be in the area, so Mary would be able to make plans for a visit, often traveling back with them. The two Marys formed a special bond because of their love for Jesus. They would sit and talk for hours about the things He had said, what they had learned from it, and the difference it was making in the way they saw things.

thirteen

MARY BECAME MORE AND MORE ALARMED AS TIME PASSED AND she noticed the tide of public opinion going first for Jesus and then against Him.

"They have no stability. They're just like stupid sheep. They will follow whoever is in the lead with the strongest voice. What chance does He have of raising an army if they won't stand solidly behind Him?"

For the first time, doubts started coming into her mind. "Is He really the deliverer promised by God? He doesn't seem to be in any hurry to overthrow the government."

Little bursts of anger and frustration came to the forefront. She decided that the next time He was in the area, she would talk to Him, reminding Him of what He was supposed to be doing.

When she heard He was heading for Jerusalem, she told Hannah that she had to go see Him. Reuben made arrangements with some neighbors who were traveling at the same time. She rehearsed in her mind the whole time they were walking exactly what she would say. She would tell Him that while He was popular for the miracles He had performed, He had better get His army together. He should stop wasting time and energy and get busy with what He was sent to do.

Her first glimpse of Him was through the crowd that seemed to be always surrounding Him. He was talking to them, answering their questions. Some of His answers were startling to Mary. He spoke about them trying to kill Him and talked as though He was going to die.

Mary heard the people around her whispering to each other. Some were agreeing that it was time to put an end to His ranting; others were beginning to believe that He was the Messiah. As He spoke, Mary realized with a clarity sent from God that Jesus' kingdom was not going to be on the earth. Her heart grabbed in her chest, and she could hardly breathe as the reality settled in.

The murmuring grew louder and more belligerent. People were even picking up stones to throw at Jesus. Mary's mouth went dry in fear. She had to get to her son, but when she tried to push through the crowd, Jesus had disappeared.

Mary made her way out of the temple court, much shaken. Slowly she proceeded, alone, out of the city and began the walk toward Bethany. Maybe Jesus had gone there. Thoughts churned through her mind. Could she hide Him? How could she bear to see her son, her firstborn, be killed? Was that really what God intended from the beginning? She wanted to scream and cry to God to spare Him, but something held her back. A memory of their first visit to the temple with Jesus flashed into her mind. The old man at the temple had told her a sword would pierce her soul. Is this what he meant?

Tears flowed down her cheeks. Her knees would no longer hold her. She found a rock beside the road and sat for a while to regain her strength and composure.

"O God, how could You ask this of me? He's my son, flesh of my flesh. I cannot face this!"

A warm presence enveloped her. The reassuring voice of God, audible only to her spirit, spoke. "He is also My Son. I love Him too. I will be with you through this. You don't have to face it alone. This is not the end."

She sat silently, soaking up the comfort of His presence, thinking about the words she had heard. In the midst of her pondering came the thought, *What did He mean, it's not the end?* She decided that in His own time, He would allow her to understand.

Finally she made her way to the home of Lazarus, Mary and Martha. Lazarus was sitting on a bench outside the door, and Martha was fussing over him, trying to get him to take a drink. Mary came out the door with a wet cloth and placed it on his head.

"I think he needs to lie down," Mary suggested to the sisters. Martha ran ahead to prepare the sleeping mat while the two Marys helped him to his feet and made their way into the house.

Mary stayed with them overnight, helping them as they cared for their dearly loved brother. They all knew he was very ill. Although unspoken, the thought was in all their minds that if Jesus was there, He would be able to heal him.

Finally Martha asked, "Where is Jesus? Have you seen Him?"

With a thump that Mary was sure they would be able to hear, her heart fell. She had momentarily forgotten the scene in the temple court. She took a deep breath, swallowed and answered. "He was in the temple in Jerusalem, but He disappeared. I don't know where He went."

In the early light of day, Mary set off once more for Hannah and Reuben's home outside Jericho. This time she was in company of one of Mary and Martha's neighbors, who was trying to find Jesus for them. Mary was quiet as they began their journey toward Jericho. She was troubled about the changing situation with Jesus and concerned over Lazarus. The neighbor was not well-known to her, so she didn't feel that she could confide in him, but at this point she was not ready to confide in anyone. She had to be able to get her thoughts into words before she could share them.

The farther she walked, the more she thought; the more she thought, the faster she walked. Her thoughts were running over each other like sheep. To slow herself down and stop her runaway mind, she looked at the young man who was with her. His eyes were downcast, studying the road at his feet. His face was clean-shaven—a man not yet married. How did he feel, being guardian to an older woman? Would he rather have been somewhere else?

As if feeling her eyes upon him, the young man, named Jacob, looked at Mary. His eyes were dark with concern. "I think it's time to take a rest," he said.

"I'm not tired yet," Mary replied.

Jacob smiled. "That's the point. We rest before we get tired; then we can travel farther."

As they made themselves as comfortable as they could on the stones beside the road, Jacob spoke again. "How well do you know Lazarus and his sisters?"

"They're very good friends of ours. We've visited often in the past years. They have been such an encouragement to Jesus and, because of that, such an encouragement to me. I would do anything for them."

Jacob smiled, but his eyes filled with tears. "I owe my life to them, and to Jesus. I was ready to kill myself until they let me know I was a worthwhile human being. I was ill with leprosy and had no hope of recovery until Jesus healed me. He just put His hand on my head and prayed, and the illness left. It has not come back. Even after that, some people are afraid to come near me. Lazarus and his sisters provide my meals and lodging, and Lazarus has found work for me to do so I can support myself, but they're still making sure I'm looked after until I have the strength and confidence to be on my own. I, too, would do anything for them. That is why I offered to go find Jesus for them. I know He can heal. I have experienced it. I know He loves them as well. I just hope I can find Him in time." He looked off toward the eastern horizon, and a tear slipped down his cheek.

Mary reached out and placed her hand on his, squeezing it lightly. Jacob flinched but did not pull away.

He explained, "I still sometimes think of myself as being unclean around those who don't know me well. I want to protect them if they come too close."

Mary's hand tightened on his. "How long has it been since Jesus healed you?"

"Just a few weeks. I expect I will get used to it in time, but after five years of being unclean…"

Mary's mother heart contracted. This man was so young. He would have been no more than a child when he was stricken and would not have been allowed physical contact with anyone. She reached out and took his face between her hands as her own eyes filled with tears. Then she pulled him toward her and enveloped him in a warm, loving, motherly hug.

A single sob escaped him before he pulled himself together. "It's time to be on our way again."

Mary smiled. He would be fine. He was strong; he was well. After all, the Messiah had healed him.

They talked easily as they continued on their way. He asked her how Jesus was able to heal, and she told him the whole story, from the appearance of the angel right to His disappearance at the temple the day before.

"You mean, I was healed by the Messiah? The Son of the Most High God?" His voice trembled. "Why? I mean, why me?"

"Because He loves you. Because you are important to Him. Because you have a work to do for Him. But mostly because He loves you."

Jacob lifted his hands and looked toward heaven with tears raining down his cheeks. "I don't completely understand, God, but I thank You!" Then he dropped to his knees, offering himself to God, to use in any way He saw fit.

He rose from his knees, turning to Mary. He began bowing before her, but she grasped his hands.

"No! I'm only a human being like you. Give your adoration to God, not to me."

"But you're the mother of the Most High God!"

"I'm the mother of God's Son. I am only a human vessel. There's nothing holy about me."

Jacob stood up. "Forgive me," he whispered.

Mary smiled at him. "Of course I forgive you. I wonder how many times I have had to say that to God during my life. If I was holy, I wouldn't have to do that, now would I?"

Jacob returned her smile, and they resumed walking. A short distance farther on they could see the outline of the buildings on the edge of Jericho.

"Come with me to my daughter's home. They may have heard something that will lead you to Jesus."

Reuben and Hannah were able to tell Jacob that Jesus and His followers had passed through Jericho only the night before. Jesus told them they would be traveling on to Bethany, beyond the Jordan, for a few days. They invited Jacob to spend the night, but he said his errand was urgent and he must be on his way. He did agree to stay for a meal and to take extra food with him. He was captivated by young Sarah and her antics as she tried to look after her baby brother, and he promised to stop in on his way back to Lazarus.

By the time Mary had the opportunity to talk freely with Hannah, she had her thoughts and emotions in order, and she was able to relate the events in Jerusalem without showing the panic and heart-stopping fear she had felt when they had happened. She realized that the condition of Lazarus and the encounter with Jacob had made her realize how small her own concerns were in light of the whole world, who needed the touch of her son. She still shrank from the thoughts of His possible death, but she knew that God was in control and would not allow Jesus to suffer without cause. She remembered again Joseph's words on the way back home after their first visit to the temple. "Why should He suffer when there is no real need?" If His earthly father had loved Him that much, certainly His Heavenly Father would do no less.

fourteen

THE NEXT EVENING JACOB APPEARED ALONE AT THE DOOR OF Reuben's home.

"Were you not able to find Jesus?" Mary asked.

"I found Him and gave Him the message. He said Lazarus will not die, and He will come in His time."

Jacob spent the night with them and then set out at first light. Mary was sorry she was not able to go with him, but she was still tired from her last trip and needed time to regain her energy. When she expressed her regret to Hannah, her daughter laughed.

"Do you think it's a hardship to me to have you here? Sarah adores you and will do anything you ask. You have such a way with her, and you tend baby Reuben when my arms feel like they're ready to fall off. You bring news from the outside world that I am hungry to hear. Reuben talks to me, but only about things that interest him. While we were growing up you were always so busy with the things that needed doing, you just didn't have much time to sit and talk to us individually. I really enjoy our visits. Reuben has often mentioned how much more relaxed I am when you're here. Take as long as you like to rest from your journey. I'm not in a hurry to have you leave."

The next few days were, indeed, restful for Mary. Sarah's busyness kept her mind occupied. When she held baby

Reuben, cuddling him close, it reminded her of her firstborn son so many years before. She had had no responsibilities except him, and she recalled the hours she spent holding Him, talking to Him, loving Him. She reluctantly passed Reuben back to Hannah at feeding times, allowing herself to be brought back to the present by an ever-present inquisitive little Sarah.

When word came that Lazarus had died, she was shocked. Jesus had said he wouldn't die. They all went immediately to be with Mary and Martha, to give them what comfort they could. Mary felt she was unable to give anything when her heart was so empty. How could Jesus be wrong? How was Jacob feeling? Did he feel betrayed? Was his faith intact? Had he told Mary and Martha what Jesus had said?

As they came near the house, they could see the crowd of friends surrounding it. Did they all know that Jesus had lied to them? Mary didn't have the strength right then to go any farther. "Reuben, give me a chance to catch my breath," she said. "You go ahead without me. I'll be along later."

Hannah looked sharply at her mother. "Are you all right? Do you feel sick?"

"I just need some time alone. Don't worry about me. I will come when I'm ready."

She watched as Reuben and Hannah and the little ones approached the house. A short time later she saw a figure coming toward her. As he neared, she saw that it was Jacob. She stood to greet him.

To her surprise, he was smiling. "It's good to see you again!" he exclaimed.

Mary was taken aback. "Didn't you say Jesus told you Lazarus wouldn't die?" She blurted out the question with no thought of how it would sound.

"Yes. That is what He said, and I still believe Him. He's God's Son, remember?"

"But Lazarus is dead."

"Right now he is, but Jesus isn't here yet."

Mary thought about his words and his faith. She thought about the many times through the years when God had accomplished the impossible. A small glimmer of light began to shine in her soul. "Have you said anything to Mary and Martha about it?"

"Yes, but they can't see beyond the grave."

"And you can?"

"In this case, yes. And so can you. I can see it beginning to grow in you. Oh, Mary, I was dead, and He brought me back to life."

"But you weren't in the grave."

"My soul was. I think that's worse. Nothing is impossible for God!"

"I want to believe you're right, but I'm afraid."

"Did Jesus ever lie to you?"

"No."

Jacob reached out and took her by the shoulders. "Then why would He start now?"

Mary laughed—a joyful, relieved, believing laugh. She put her hands on Jacob's chest and bowed her head. "O God, I thank You for Jacob and for his wonderful faith in You. I thank You for sending him to be your answer for my weak faith. Comfort Mary and Martha. Help them to believe as well."

Side by side, they walked to the house. It was some time before Mary was able to get to Martha and her sister. Because of the crowd and the mourning and wailing, she was unable to say anything. She gave each of them a warm hug, just letting them know she cared so very much for them.

After the brief visit and a trip to Lazarus's tomb, they began the journey back to Jericho. Jacob traveled part of the way with them. Before they were halfway there, they met Jesus and His close followers. They greeted each other and then went on their respective ways.

Jacob turned around and went back toward Bethany with Jesus. Mary knew she would have an account of the happenings from him later. She smiled when she thought about him. She knew he would not be able to stay with the group but would likely run on ahead to tell them Jesus was coming.

She was not surprised two days later to hear Jacob's voice at the door. She ran to meet him, drawing him inside where Reuben and Hannah were sitting.

"Tell us!" she exclaimed.

His face shone as he recounted the events of the day. "Jesus came! He went to the tomb and called for Lazarus to come out. And he came! Do you know what I think? I think He had to call Lazarus by name so *everyone* who was dead didn't come out of their graves! He's that powerful! Now Lazarus is back at home with Mary and Martha. They are so full of joy and gladness, they can hardly contain it! You should have seen Martha tearing around getting things for everybody to eat. And Mary was staring at Lazarus as though she had never seen such a beautiful sight, as though she couldn't get enough of looking at him."

Reuben asked, "What was the reaction of the people?"

"About what you would expect. There are many who believe He is the Messiah, but there are others who just get angrier. He is upsetting their tidy little lives, and they don't like it."

Reuben shook his head. "Lazarus is well-known and well-liked. They aren't going to be able to ignore this. They knew he was dead, and now he is alive. How will they explain their anger over that?"

"They will find some way. They'll lie if they can't find another way, or they'll pay somebody else to lie."

Mary quietly put everyone's fears into words. "It really isn't safe for Him in Jerusalem anymore." Then she added, "Passover is coming. He always goes to Jerusalem for Passover." The now familiar cold hand gripped her heart.

A few days later, Jesus Himself came to Reuben and Hannah's home. He told them He was spending some time in Jericho before going on to Jerusalem for the Passover. It was as Mary had feared. She decided then that He would not be making this journey without her. She didn't know what she could do for Him, but she would be there.

She spent unforgettable days in His presence, observing His kindness to those who were ill, listening to His teaching for those who would listen. Most memorable was the encounter with the hated and feared Zacchaeus, a Jewish man who had, in the opinion of the townspeople, sold out to the Romans. He collected hard-earned money from his own people and sent it to Rome. At least, some of it went to Rome. He was wealthy, most said from the money he stole from the people of the area. But Jesus stopped to talk to him, to invite Himself to Zacchaeus' home, and there a miracle had happened. Zacchaeus had promised to restore anything he had taken illegally four times over! He also pledged to give away half of what he had to help the poor. Of course there were skeptics. Even Mary had to own to a feeling of "I'll believe that when I see it."

A week before Passover, Jesus told His mother He was leaving for Bethany. Mary and Martha wanted to give a supper in His honor to thank him for giving Lazarus back to them.

"May I come along with you, if I promise not to interfere?"

Jesus smiled, but His eyes held a sadness that she had never before seen. His answer stayed with her through the rest of her life. "Yes, Mother, I would appreciate having you with Me."

Mary assured Hannah that she would be back after the Passover celebrations. They traveled slowly because of the crowds of people who now flocked around Jesus wherever He went. He talked to them, listened to them, touched and healed many, but always managed to let Mary know He was aware of her presence. If the road became rough, His hand was on her arm to help her along; if she grew weary, He encouraged her with a smile or just a brief glance.

As soon as they arrived at the home of Lazarus, Mary went inside to help in the preparations for the meal while Jesus and His disciples remained outside, talking to the people who had come with them. Mary and Martha joyfully greeted Mary. Martha gave her a flour-covered hug and then apologized while trying to clean the front of her garments.

"Don't be concerned about it. It will clean. I'll look worse by the time the meal is finished," Mary assured her. They laughed and began working together. When the guests started to arrive, they were kept very busy seeing that the serving platters remained full.

Mary was suddenly aware of the most beautiful fragrance she had ever smelled. She looked toward Martha. "What is that lovely smell?"

They entered the room where the feast was taking place. Mary was on her knees before Jesus, wiping His feet with her hair, a small jar on the floor beside her. Her deed had caused quite a stir in the room. Martha was about to reprimand her, but Mary placed her hand lightly on Martha's mouth. Her eyes filled with tears as she recognized the love and gratitude in Mary's actions.

Some of the disciples were talking among themselves. One of them, Judas, spoke his displeasure.

"This is a terrible waste! That perfume is expensive. It could have been sold and the money used to help the poor. A year's wages would help a lot of people."

Mary held her breath. She wasn't worried that Jesus would misunderstand; she was concerned about what the others would think of Mary.

"Leave her alone," Jesus said. "She is preparing My body for burial. The poor will be here whenever you want to do something for them. I will not be."

"Preparing My body for burial"? Mary thought. *What is He talking about?* She needed to get out somewhere by herself to think, to pray, to scream if necessary.

She stepped outside and stopped. There were crowds of people surrounding the house, with more coming all the time.

Someone close to her asked, "Is Jesus inside? We came to see Him."

She went back into the house to pass along the message, and then she slipped away behind the house to talk to God. "O God, I'm scared! I have so many confused thoughts in my mind. I know You have all the answers, but I don't think I want to know what they are right now. You said Jesus would save His people from their sins. For us that has always meant sacrificing a goat or a lamb."

Into her mind came the words of John the Baptist at the Jordan River: "Look, the Lamb of God, who takes away the sin of the world!"

Her knees gave out, and she dropped to the ground. "You're going to allow them to sacrifice my son?" she asked incredulously.

She couldn't stand the pain of her thoughts, so she stumbled into the house to get away from them. Martha was bustling around, putting things away and cleaning up. Her sister Mary looked toward her, reading some of the agony and confusion, and came to her with a comforting hug.

"What's the problem?" she asked quietly.

Mary just shook her head.

Martha called to her sister for help moving some of the things back into their places, and Mary was left alone.

Isn't there anyone else? Before the thought was completely formed, she knew the answer. It was for this reason He had come into the world. He was the only one. He was perfect. He was God. He was born to be the sacrifice for His people.

When? How? Her thoughts were racing again. The Passover Lamb, sacrificed on the altar. His blood sprinkled on the doorposts.

Does He know already? She knew the answer to that as well. Now she understood the reason for the sadness in His eyes.

"O, God, how can I bear this?" Mary slipped outside again to walk, to be alone.

It was near dawn when she heard footsteps behind her. She turned to see Jesus coming. Neither of them spoke as He enveloped her in His arms. They stood in silence for many minutes, and then He spoke softly. "I'm going to Jerusalem for the Passover celebration. I want you to stay here with Mary and Martha."

She nodded without speaking. She knew that in her present state of mind she would be an added burden to Him. She asked no questions. She made no requests. She didn't even assure Him of her love. He knew, and she didn't want to take away from His intense concentration on doing the will of His Father.

Before He left, He looked into her eyes.

She thought, *When can I come to You?*

Without anyone speaking, she received her answer. *You will know.*

Then He was gone. She refused to watch Him go.

She stayed by herself most of the day and was very quiet, even when Mary and Martha were around. Mary seemed to understand and respected her privacy. Martha, in her own way, did the same, but it was more by ignoring the fact of her presence, except for having food available if she should want or need it.

Two days later, early in the morning, Jacob arrived, ashen-faced, to tell them that Jesus had been arrested the night before and had gone to trial. Mary went with Jacob back into Jerusalem. He led her to the palace. There was a sea of people in the courtyard. A man, whom Jacob told her was Pilate, the Roman governor, was just coming out. He raised his voice to be heard by everyone.

"This man has done no wrong. I cannot charge him. Here he is."

Mary strained to see over the heads of the crowd. She saw a man dressed in purple, with what looked like thorns around His head. His face was badly disfigured from beating, and blood ran from the places on His forehead where the thorns had broken the flesh. She didn't recognize Him until she caught the phrase "Son of God."

This being beside the governor was her son. She clutched Jacob for support lest her knees fail her again.

The two figures disappeared for a time and then reappeared. The governor was presenting Him to them as their king.

To Mary's horror she heard the words "Crucify Him!"

They wanted to hang her perfect son on a cross?

"O God, no, not that way," she whispered.

Jacob's arm went around her to support her. He led her aside to a place where she could sit down.

She glanced toward the palace as a group of soldiers took Jesus away. "We must follow them," she whispered fiercely.

"Would that be wise?"

"Is what they're doing wise?" she retorted.

Jacob helped her to her feet, and they followed the crowd as it crawled its way through the streets and out of the city. At times they would try to push their way closer to Jesus, but they were always held back. From time to time they would hear laughter and jeering ahead of them.

A sob beside her made Mary turn her head. Jacob was wiping his sleeve across his eyes.

"Do they know what they're doing? Just a few days ago they were singing praises to Him and declaring that He was their king, and now they're going to kill Him. He's so kind. He heals the sick; He feeds the hungry; He cares about them. He even raises the dead! Don't they care about that? What are they thinking?"

Mary reached for his hand, and they walked the rest of the way with their hands clasped.

By the time they arrived at the hill, the soldiers had Jesus and two criminals stretched out on their crosses. The criminals were cursing and struggling as the soldiers fought to pin them in place until the nails could be driven through their hands and feet. Jesus lay silently, allowing them to do what they would to Him. Mary winced as the first hammer blows fell. Then she covered her ears to block out the screams of the other two men.

The expression of pain on Jesus' face as they dropped the cross into place stayed with her for the rest of her life, but she wouldn't look away. She sank to the ground, watching her son as He struggled to breathe. He was naked for all to see, this Son of hers who was also the Son of God. He was the tiny newborn baby whom the shepherds had come to see; He was the older baby who had drawn the men from the east to come with their gifts and their worship; He was the toddler who had learned to walk and talk with her love and nurturing; He was the little boy who was so kind to His siblings and so obedient to His parents; He was the young man who conscientiously studied to know His Father's will; He was the man who had healed the sick, raised the dead, cleansed the lepers, fed the multitudes and so patiently taught the ones who wanted to learn. Now it was all coming to an end.

She felt a hand on her shoulder and looked around. John, one of her son's closest and dearest friends, stood beside her and Jacob. Mary reached up and took his hand for a brief squeeze and then let her hand drop back to her lap.

The mocking continued as Jesus hung there on the cross. Mary could hear quiet comments about His claims to be God's Son. Then a voice would ring out, loud enough for Jesus to hear, "You think You're so great! Save Yourself. Come down off the cross and prove that what You are saying is so!" At such times there would be derisive laughter from different areas of the gathered crowd.

Each time Jesus spoke, the people were silent, trying to hear what He was saying. Once he looked directly at Mary and John and spoke to them, giving His mother into the care of John.

"Even now He is looking after me!" she sobbed.

John knelt beside Mary and placed his arms around her as she cried.

Through the long hours, many people came to speak quietly to Mary, to offer comfort by a touch of a hand or a hug. She was aware that they were coming but let nothing distract her from the form of her son, suffering more intensely now as He struggled to breathe.

For Mary, one of the worst moments was when Jesus cried out, wondering why His Father had forsaken Him. For His sake she remained silent, but her heart was torn and she wanted to scream at God to do something—anything!

The sky grew dark. Uneasiness infected the onlookers. They huddled closer together, muttering about judgment. Even the soldiers looked warily around them.

Suddenly, Jesus cried out in a voice loud enough to be heard by all around, "It is finished!" His head fell forward, and Mary knew He was dead.

The ground trembled, and some of the nearby rocks split apart.

A pain Mary had never before experienced went through her. She felt totally alone, like there was no one anywhere she could turn to. Even God was silent.

The activity around her increased. She realized there were people wrapping Jesus' body for burial. She knelt beside the lifeless body of her firstborn, too spent to even cry. She reached out and touched His face, hardly recognizable as the son she had known and loved with all her heart. She studied the body with detachment, until she looked at His hands. Her head rested on the wounded hand she held between her own, and sobs shook her again. Those hands that had never hurt but always cared for and healed and loved were torn and pierced by the nails that had held Him to the cross.

John was beside her, gently removing Jesus' hand from hers, enfolding her in his arms as her consciousness began slipping away. Strong arms lifted her. She was carried some distance and laid on a bed. For hours she lay in an agony so intense she wanted to die. Her son was gone…her light, her life, her hope.

She was dimly aware of people around her, but nothing mattered. As consciousness began to return she saw Martha sitting beside her, offering her a drink. When she had swallowed as much as she wanted, Martha took the cup and stayed with her until she dropped off to sleep.

The next few days passed in a blur. She was by turns numb, then angry, then unbelievably sad.

Early one morning she was awakened by a commotion. Mary Magdalene, whom Jesus had delivered from demons, came into the house crying.

"His body is gone. They have taken it!"

Mary sat up, thinking she was dreaming. Mary Magdalene was standing there with tears running down her face. Her hair was windblown, and she was out of breath.

John and Peter, who was also staying at the house, ran to check out her story and find Jesus' body if they could. A short time later they returned, downcast.

"His body is gone," John told her. "But we will find it."

They sat talking about what could have happened. Had they gone to the wrong tomb? Had the authorities taken His body away? As they talked, Mary returned, breathless as before. This time she was smiling as the tears poured down her cheeks.

"He's alive! I saw Him. I talked to Him. He told me to tell you."

They looked at each other in disbelief. She turned to Jesus' mother.

"I'm telling you the truth! I wouldn't make this up."

Mary studied her face. It was alight with a joy that could not have been faked. But was she insane? Unbidden came the memory of the day she saw the angel at the well. Her mother had thought she was insane. She stood and embraced the other Mary, whispering, "I want to believe you, but I'm so afraid."

Mary Magdalene returned the hug, saying nothing.

Later that day they were together, discussing the possibilities of what had happened and what to do next. Then Jesus was there with them. He showed them His hands. They were speechless for a few moments, then burst forth with joy and praises to God.

He stood before His mother. "You don't have to be afraid any more. I'm here. I am alive."

Joy and relief flooded through Mary. She wrapped her arms around her son and held on as though she would never let go. He rested His head against hers as He returned the hug. Then He released her.

The next few weeks were times of upheaval and change as Mary and the other disciples came to the realization that Jesus had actually conquered death. He had paid for their sin, once for all. There would be no more need of sacrifices; there was no need for the high priest to be their mediator before God. All the things Jesus had told them and taught them began to make sense. They asked Him innumerable questions when He was with them and discussed His answers when He wasn't.

One day as He was talking to them, He began rising from the ground. They watched without speaking until a cloud hid Him from their view. Still they stood staring. Mary became aware of a shimmering light; then two men in white stood with them. They told the gathered group that Jesus had gone to heaven but would someday return.

With the promise of the angels echoing in their minds, they returned to the city, where they spent much time in prayer waiting for the Holy Spirit, as Jesus had told them.

Mary sat slightly apart from the group on one occasion, talking to God as she had so many times through her life. She asked forgiveness for the anger she had felt and for the lack of trust she had exhibited.

"And now it is over," she whispered.

Very clearly, the answer came back. "It has only begun."